T0319218

Kinsmen of the President

Edlyne Ezenongaya Anugwom

Langaa Research & Publishing CIG
Mankon, Bamenda

Publisher:
Langaa RPCIG
Langaa Research & Publishing Common Initiative Group
P.O. Box 902 Mankon
Bamenda
North West Region
Cameroon
Langaagrp@gmail.com
www.langaa-rpcig.net

Distributed in and outside N. America by African Books Collective
orders@africanbookscollective.com
www.africanbookscollective.com

ISBN: 9956-763-51-9

© Edlyne Ezenongaya Anugwom 2016

All rights reserved.
No part of this book may be reproduced or transmitted in any form or by
any means, mechinal or electronic, including photocopying and recording,
or be stored in any information storage or retrieval system, without
written permission from the publisher

DISCLAIMER
All views expressed in this publication are those of the author and do not
necessarily reflect the views of Langaa RPCIG.

Before It All Began

*F**riday is an important day for me as I craft the final version of my page five article for the weekend edition of the paper. Saturday papers are popular, especially among the middle class who do not work on Saturdays and can enjoy the bumper editions which carry an overview of the week's all important news and events; sports round – up (a pull out of four pages in most serious newspapers); and a loaded celebrity gossip section which caters to the mundane taste of upper class housewives, wannabes, and spinsters with eyes on prosperous partners. In fact, every reader wins on a Saturday.*

Given this fact which has adequate but yet unpublished statistical backing, I aim at doing my best with my Saturday article and the fact that it usually gets triple the number of readers' reaction and often rejoinders than any other outing of mine validates the, "Saturday is Prime" hypothesis. On this particular Friday I was busy running through my article for the Saturday edition as the hustle and clatter of the newsroom suggested the usual emptying of the place in the next one hour. It was true what they say, 'Thank Goodness it's Friday'.

There is usually a magic to Friday as people turn up to work overtly friendly, chirpy and easy-going. This was the demeanour brought about by the expectation of a work-free two days of the weekend. I had carefully observed the work attitudes and demeanour of people on the major days of the week – Monday, Wednesday, and Friday. Mondays are usually serious days and people confront their tasks with renewed energy, make work plans for the week, and are extra mindful of rules. Wednesdays are marked as more or less routine days; people grind through their tasks often at a slower pace than usual and a noticeable dulling of movements and body language takes over in most people. However, Fridays are special since the mornings are like a repeat of Mondays although people are more friendly and chatty. However, the afternoons resemble Wednesdays though the chirpy nature remains intact and people avoid tasking and time consuming work chores. Friday is magical indeed.

I was still poring through the final version of the article having made a few corrections and additions here and there based on the observations of a key member of the editorial board who had emailed the article as an attached file to me an hour ago. My usual practice is to have the Saturday article ready in draft form before mid-day on Thursday and then send it electronically to my favourite member of the editorial board for his comments before I work out the final version by late Friday afternoon. This arrangement has worked for a good period now.

My favourite board member is a reclusive university professor of strategic studies and cultural diversity who would rather spend eternity with a book and in a library than with any other entity and anywhere else. I glanced up from the article towards the air conditioner vents; the place had become a little hot in spite of the best efforts of the aged air conditioning system. It was over 30 degree outside and I could feel the sweat gathering around my forehead and my Fruit of the Loom singlet was beginning to get stuck to my back. I quickly adjusted my position and bent down once more to go through the last paragraph of the revised article.

It was an article titled, "Human Rights Abuses and Overflowing Jails", which criticized the growing penchant of the military dictators in power to load the prisons with all sorts of people on the flimsiest of excuses especially those who are politically opinionated; overtly critical of the government and its henchmen; and even human rights and environmental activists. In the article I pointed out how this development constitutes gross abuse of human rights, endangers the health of these political prisoners who go through hell in the country's hellish prison system; and how this practice of jail your critics before they talk was indiscriminate and did not fathom in any consideration of social status, including one's ethnic or religious standing, two factors usually considered seriously in public life in the country.

I ended the piece by revealing that even the kinsmen of the apex military dictator in power were not spared this ordeal once they step out of the arbitrary line drawn by the military. As a result of the comments and suggestions of the reclusive professor, I had changed the title of the final version to "Kinsmen of the President – the deepening contrasts of power" which even though I felt sounded too intellectual, seemed catchy enough and cut to the heart of the matter.

One: Caged

It is funny but I guess I must start somewhere. My story might make you laugh; it might broaden your imagination, or at least raise your wrath against faceless institutions in the society, especially in those societies still engrossed in catching up with the rest or is it the West. But before you allow any of them to seize you, hear me out.

Have you ever been arrested? Well, maybe you have not, but do you know or can you imagine what it means to be arrested? From my own corner of the universe an arrest can be effected anywhere, anytime. Well, you might have been arrested by the local policemen for fighting or causing obstruction or one other of the irrelevancies that fill the criminal and anti-social sections of our constitution (if we still have something like that). But few people ever panic when they are accosted by the local policemen. This is because of the nature of that arm of the security forces.

In Naija, whatever your crime is, even murder can be bought off the police. With enough influence and money, somebody can kill in this country and get away with it. Quite a significant number of people known to me and unknown have done it repeatedly. Moreover, the flat footed policemen are people we see every day, we commune with them and sometimes sleep with them as fellow citizens or relatives. Basically, the only myths about them are not their uniform or their talent, but their guns and the countless number of laws they flaunt at people. Hence, they are first and foremost people we can identify with and share their universe or existence.

They are part and parcel of everyday frustration of living. Their ubiquitous nature and their now popular beggarly attitudes towards the public have made them almost less than

5

ordinary. Whether clad in grey khaki or blue-grayish khaki or whatever drab colours suit the imagination of those who clothe them; they are people we are used to and most times bored with. The wife battering records of those of them in public yards or the popular "face - me, I – face – you"(or what my best friend calls: "face-me, I – slap - you" in reference to both the violence and climate of conflict in such dwellings dignified by the estate feat of putting maximum humanity in minimum unfit accommodation) accommodations; their scruffy uniforms; scrawny or pot-bellied frames; and tattered shoes stick out as edifices to their fall from colonial grace to today's post-colonial grass. In fact, a colleague once commented that any residual respect he had for policemen evaporated with their first change of uniform.

But have you been arrested by the gendarmes or other faceless and heartless mufti-clad operatives of the state security service? It is then you would know the full weight of arrest. It hits one like a wild engulfing cyclone. An arrest is a terrible gap in somebody's life. It is an adverse and pervasive intrusion into one's life. There are no preliminaries to arrest in the hands of these operatives; you certainly become confused, benumbed and in a state of shock for a long time. Only a few people and some of them veterans of the state apparatus of repression are able to coherently inquire why the sudden clamp. But silence is the response from these men; perhaps an inverse case of silence is golden.

Sometimes they do volunteer information but such information doesn't answer the question – why am I being arrested? Their answers vary between three points; you will know when we get to the office; my superior wants to see you; your help is needed. Either way, these mindless operatives answer by rote. It is a routine reply when they feel like it.

Such innocent chores needed from you. No big deal, your

mind seems to argue. You will be back soon enough. But why are they armed to the teeth with snub-nosed revolvers, or more likely their ubiquitous Mark 4; and why cut you off from your physical and social environment so abruptly. You are not given the liberty to tell anyone, to phone somebody, to take something or to change clothes. After all, it wouldn't be doing your image any good if you are hustled into detention in your three piece suit or elongated corporate tie.

But why worry, after all these are gentlemen and would be as good as their word. Not at all, if there is anything they need from you like incriminating papers, they get for themselves. Anything written down these days right from an obituary to a pen pal request can be incriminating in this country. So long as those that make and wield power want it so.

Like a lamb you obey their instructions and follow them. Given the accidental discharge proneness of our security services you have no other reasonable option. But there is always an aura of the cryptic and clandestine about the activities of these agents of the state. In all the stories I have heard while behind the clamper they usually get you when you have no witness at all, they don't advertise the fact. You are to be taken away surreptitiously and you are not expected to make noise. Those that tried refusing the overtures of these men found out the hard way how asinine it was.

While in detention I compared notes with other inmates on how they got to be there of all enviable places. One thing became obvious to me. More than three quarters of those behind bars are not quite sure of their offences. They are interrogated and found culpable on yarns spun by the interrogators. As a matter of reliable conjecture, before the security personnel come for you, they have a built up a case against you. Whether true, silly or fabricated, interrogation becomes a sullied routine, geared towards bending you to what they consider within the confines of their regimented brains unassailable facts against you.

By the time they are through with the duel called interrogation, you will gladly sign a confession (don't bother telling the judge it was signed under duress). Most times you are never brought to court. You are tortured and humiliated as long as desired and then released. And only few people successfully resist singing one song or another in confession. By the way, the confession is written or rather composed by them. Your duty is to copy this into another sheet of paper and scrawl a signature beneath it. Many of the people that refused to comply have one scar or the other that they will take to the grave with them.

Many people don't come out of their dungeons complete as they went in. You either lose an eye, an ear, a limb or contract one terminal ailment or another that you would always celebrate in remembrance of the unlucky few that perished inside. Actually, I once wrote an article for a general interest magazine entitled, "Beyond Prison Demographics" in which I argued that demographic outlook is in disfavor of those who have spent any reasonable length of time in our prison facilities.

It was one of those articles which drew simply on observation of the death pattern especially among the yesteryears politicians, a good number of who had spent years in the gallows as guests of the uniformed usurpers who drove them out of office. I reported that a look at those politicians who had spent about three to five years in prison before being granted pardon shows that about half of them died within three years of release while another half of those still alive are in the clutches of several health ailments that look sure to take them to the world beyond. By this time I had not imagined that a nice guy like me would be in a place like that.

8

Anyhow, if you are not a big fish or popular, dying in detention is a big odd. And if you exasperate Mr. President by volunteering to die in detention, then you would be given a state burial. Relatives are neither informed nor invited. A few Nijans missing from the over 150 million others wouldn't raise alarms especially if they miss secretly. The United Nations Fund for Population might even send flowers.

The mode of arresting people varies but they have one thing in common - the secrecy. Look at the following ways of uprooting people from their milieu. The human rights activist, Shehu Mamman stopped a taxi in front of his apartment block one grey Saturday morning. The taxi stopped and picked him up. Shehu was going to the theatre. On the way, the taxi driver told him he would make a detour to avoid a hold-up. Innocently Shehu agreed. There was nothing fishy in that. The street which linked the residential areas easily with the city commercial centre was usually busy. En route the driver stopped and picked up two more passengers. That was all. Shehu Mamman without least expecting it became a guest of the state. Mamman had been engaged in a serious pro-democracy drive against the totalitarian military regime.

He was on the eve of launching a major offensive the next week with his collaborators. Four of his collaborators were also separately picked up that Saturday morning. They had all planned to meet in the theatre and iron out their strategies while watching a drama presentation. It was always difficult to converse over the five rows of seat, what with the din of the drama and the hostile glances of spectators who will feel disturbed by their hushed voices.

But against the back drop of constant state surveillance and incessant stalking, a little ingenuity and discomfort might be stomached. Their arrest had thrown spanners into the works. Once more, the government's privy to superior monitoring and coercive apparatus had won.

What of the case of Sarah Finih, the student union leader? Sarah was being courted unknown to her by an agent of the security services who doubled as a full time student. One day he invited her home with him and she walked into a trap. The union had gone far during her tenure due to sheer determination on her part coupled with a ferocious spirit. It was because of that that the government already had a mole in place. There was also the woman who told me of the way she was yanked off a New York bound plane and deposited at the airport base of the security services.

A fellow journalist, Bukar Ahmed, was snatched on his way to the bank one morning. The bank was just a stone throw from his newspaper office. So he was trekking the distance when a cab suddenly stopped in front of him, as he made to pass, two men climbed out of the cab. Before he could utter 'what's the matter' he had been bundled into the car with tinted windows. There were pedestrians around but they hardly got wise to what was happening.

The VIPs are given an altogether different treatment especially those who had been in favour with the government and then fell out of favour. The former oil minister, Mr. Ogasi was a case. A slight policy disagreement bordering on conflict of personal interests led to the dismissal of the entire cabinet of the all-powerful General. Instead of going home to enjoy his loot or to the ivory tower to mould ideas and characters, the don started shooting off his mouth. He became an ardent and born again critic of the government, and given his sojourn in the government, he had a lot of government's own dirty linen to wash in public.

But the government got wiser; they dusted one file off his dossier while a minister and carefully forged a foolproof case against him. The case was quite absurd, that because of the bribe of a pair of black shoes by a foreign oil contracting firm, he had over-valued and awarded a contract the firm could hardly deliver on. The state security men were sent after him; but being an important member of the community they couldn't just walk in and grab him. Not that they were afraid of anybody but they didn't want to arouse public opprobrium until they had webbed the case strongly against him and taken a decision on who to try him and what sentence to give him, so that everything would proceed promptly. So they went through his university.

At the end of lecture one day, an unfamiliar student had followed him to his office under the pretext of asking him some questions. In the office, he had barely sat down when three more people came in. They were all clad in neat gray safari with bulging breast pockets and were far from merry. They had taken him away quietly. It took the nation the better part of two months to know what happened to the crusading ex-minister. By then he had been convicted of graft while in office and given a prison term (graft that was a national past-time during that period). Now it was still the same. Only that it had gone nuclear and highly scientific. Graft was subtly encouraged by the government of General Hamid that had gained a peculiar niche for its skill in settling people.

But I am not by any stretch of the imagination a big fish or a big mouth. My only claim to fame is a regular by-line in a daily that has a circulation of little more than 175,000 a day. My job as editor of the Urban Times was by no means a fantastically well-paying job but it had its challenges. With two degrees in political science, and mass communication plus a natural flair for writing I was ready made for a newspaper career. It was my job to write the political feature of the newspaper as well as guide the process that generates the daily editorial comment.

It would amount to an overtly ego trip to describe myself as eminent whether in terms of physical or behavioural attributes. Pictures tell a thousand tales but looking into one's picture often obscures these tales or positively exaggerates them. But I remember that in the third year of my secondary school education, our English teacher asked each member of my class to write a page on the physical and behavioural attributes of his best friend in the class. The best essay turned out to be Wisdom Kayete's description of me. Till this day, this description which the teacher said neither lies nor falters has been re-echoed so many times by other people. According to him, Jerry Oldo is ebony black in complexion, rangy without being too tall, with an aquiline face, prominent eye lashes and jaw bones though endowed with overtly reddish lips given to puckishness and quivers whenever angry, embarrassed or agitated. The face rests on an average skull endowed with full hairs and undersized ears. Given to being blunt and assertive, you always know where you stand with him. However, he is prone to plucking his nostrils or leaving his mouth slightly open whenever engrossed in thought or captivated by an event.

Incidentally I have maintained these attributes except the nose plucking which rarely occurs now but the passage of time have predictably weathered these physical attributes (waning the positives and making more prominent the negatives) and sharpened the behavioural attributes. Like when I look at the mirror sometimes, I feel that the mouth is a touch too big and the ear has declined while the not too subtle lines of aging are beginning to form on one's visage. I guess we are all like that once we pass the age of thirty. I now appreciate why my mother believes that any strikingly handsome and fresh looking man at forty must be a gigolo. Thus, at a year beyond the magical forty, I was begging to show the signs of progressive physical decline.

But life begins at forty alright since beyond that number you must have seen quite a lot to avoid fatal errors and achieved enough wisdom to know that tomorrow matters, yesterday is never truly gone, and life is cyclic and enjoys the last laugh always. Ironically my ordeal here began two months after my forty-first birthday and in an oil rich country living under a military dictatorship and struggling to approach the ever receding developed nation status. This struggle had become still-born by the character of its leadership and social elites who believe in the right of might and the personalization of public offices; a tendency that creates challenges for the conscientious journalist and tasks the patience of those who believe in doing it right. In other words, the leadership exists at daggers drawn with all men and women of conscience in the country.

A situation which is even tenser when the one outside the corridors of power has the privilege of airing his opinions on the pages of a widely circulated newspaper. My craving for a better society, humane governance and the good of the greater number are the focus of my journalism. Despite these ideals, with the country enmeshed in a totalitarian military dictatorship, there were so many things to worry and even threaten a conscientious journalist.

****

The regime of General Hamid in the 1990s was a very bad one for the ordinary citizens of the nation (the amorphous band of wretches and near scum of the earth. People who have been crushed and made submissive in the tug of war of life). The economy was in shambles, there was no faith in the government any longer, the Naira was going through the journey the German currency went through once i.e. coming to the level whereby cigarette foil would be more valuable and the political class was suffering a great battering under a disemboweled; annulled; discarded; and once more nascent transition to democracy programme. A programme that was designed to confuse people and perpetuate the leadership of the military trinity in government.

The 'trinity in government' idea had gained grounds among newspaper men. It resulted from the joke a journalist cracked at the Nnamdi Azikiwe Press Center on the cabal that was in power. The trinity is seen as comprising the toothy General, the goggled General and the turbaned monarch of the North. The power base was supposed to be spearheaded by the toothy General backed up by the goggled General. Though there was an inbuilt mechanism to alternate power between the two Generals whenever there arises a need for that. In the threesome equation, the turbaned billionaire monarch performs the role of a guardian angel, making sure that things go according to the scheme of those that matter in the country. The joke had cost the impetuous newspaperman his job at the government owned Daily Times. He was lucky not to have ended up in a jailhouse as had so many helpless Nijans.

General Hamid, a tested soldier, at least by virtue of participating in a few UN peace keeping missions; some years at Sandhurst and India; and of course the mandatory barracks beer parlour obstacle course took over in a bloodless palace coup from another military regime. A regime that was on course towards rejuvenating and rehabilitating both the moral and economic status of Nijans with a serious and committed war against indiscipline and all forms of official graft and corruption. But the regime had been hastily judged by Nigerians on the basis of the facial countenance of the principal actors. So with broad smiles and charismatic personality, Hamid had soared the hopes of the citizens with

14

promises of Eldorado.

But after four years in the saddle, the General proved himself to be worse than most others, both khaki and brocade clad leaders before him.

The economy went from a tottering step to a total slumber and acute inertia. People came to appreciate suffering. Large scale repression against journalists and critics became the order of the day; those that could not be settled were repressed through the use of state security apparatus. Draconian decrees were wantonly rolled out by the expert legal draughtsman of the justice ministry to back up every whim of the government. Decrees became so numerous and encroached on all facets of public and private life that it all became a big scam. Nobody was sure of any legality again. What was legal two hours ago might be illegal after the National Network news. Not only that, decrees can also be given retrospective effect in order to entrap so called enemies of state.

Attempts were made at inducing me from government quarters but I was not in the job to make money. Even though I do not earn top notch salary I strive to keep faith with my religious beliefs. So I duly tithe, do a day per month voluntary service for the urban orphanage; keep two homeless cats I rescued from the street; and belong to the Widows and Orphans Support Club of my Diocese which involves a monthly donation of five percent of my salary to widows and orphans through the church.

I happily have not allowed the pressure of bread and butter to define my essence. I am often cast in the mold of an idealist or a medieval religious crusader by other colleagues. Forceful, consistent and uncompromising once convinced. So many other journalists have been compromised by monetary inducements. Even my 'born again' senior colleague who was in charge of the weekly Political Horoscope and formerly my

15

idol has been stained by the pervasive hue of corruption. He was hitherto a model who had spent what I thought was so many honest years in the profession. Then he was bought and changed his tunes, he made his pen blunt and his criticisms of the government less than moderate and porous. He came down some good notches in the profession but his personal economic status moved up a good many steps. He was now residing, family, dogs and all in a choice section of town; with the steering wheel of a new car in his tight grips. I was bone-'marrowy' aghast.

All my years in the field I have gotten familiar with acts of selling out on the part of journalists hence some scoops or investigative stories are snuffed out without reasons. Journalists are in a profession whereby, by commission or omission, buying their allegiance is easy. The reasons for this are not far-fetched. Every journalist in the country, except the very senior ones occupying either executive or editorial positions, is hardly well paid vis-à-vis other professionals like doctors and lawyers. Again, the country was gripped in one wave of corruption occasioned by the realities of the Hamid administration, that everybody right from toddlers to retired purblind old people was so money conscious. From my experience, one out of every thousand Nijans would reject monetary inducements not because of altruism or such other fine qualities but because the price was not fair enough according to their reckoning. Almost all Nijans have a price. Only one out of ten thousand Nijans can reject monetary inducements out of genuine ethics or personal principles.

The Friday following the eventful Saturday, I had gone to an all-night party organized for a close friend's wife who was traveling to London on a two-year in-service training course. We had rocked and grooved all night long. My friend had been blessed by God and spared no expenses in entertaining guests at the party held in his cozy residence in Ilupeju. It had lasted to the wee hours of Saturday. But on Saturday morning I was at the office. Though dead beat I had a deadline to meet. It took me about four good hours sitting in the air conditioned office and browsing through past issues of the Metropolitan to finally unwind. By the time I got to working on my article for the Monday issue other workers were leaving the office. Around 4.00pm, I went for a quiet bite at a fast food joint and came back informing the security personnel I would work late.

I had just finished my article and was dotting the I's and crossing the T's when there came a resounding knock on the door. I looked at the clock; it was some minutes after 8.00pm. Of course, fellow workers would rarely be in the office at that late hour. Was it the security men on their routine checks? But I had told them I would stay late. Before I could say come in, the door jarred open on soft hinges and four well-heeled and fine suited men came in.

"Are you Jerry Oldo?" One of the stern looking guys asked.

"That is not enough reason to barge in like that", I reprimanded in a righteously indignant tone. Looking down on my papers and with a hammering heart, I made a show of continuing my work.

Pronto, one of the men rushed upon me, collected the article I had been working on since morning and the other one started going through my shelf. I made to protest but quickly swallowed it when I came face to face with two snub nosed rifles held by the immobile twosome at the door. One of them moved forward flashed an identification card that could have belonged to the fire service or market women association and intoned in a booming voice:

"You are under arrest".

I was flustered and shocked. It did not occur to my

17

benumbed state to ask about their warrant, or to even look closely at their IDs. No. In all my years as a journalist I have always shared the credo of the risk of the profession, knowing that arrest and detention might meet the journalist on his way to work. In recent times following the assumption of office by a repressive regime, journalists have become prime targets of government security agents.

I have heard and seen cases of journalists who have been jailed under one pretense or the other for being overly critical of the government or some other well intentioned acts that go against the neo-elitist interests of the ruling class and their cronies. But I have always felt at a remote distance from such possibility. Just like we feel little or no pique when someone dies unless one close to us, I felt that going to prison or suffering the indignity of detention was something made for some others who are not so lucky, so blessed and may be so destined. Just like the issue of the disease of HIV, it seems not to exist until it gets someone very close to you. Until that hour of final realization, it would all sound like fables and at best, things made only for unfortunate casual friends and mere acquaintances.

It was not as if I had never gone near a police station before, far from it. I first experienced police cell in form four in college during a rowdy students' protest. A peaceful protest organized by form four students who were about entering their next year at college degenerated into a full scale riot. Two days before the protest, some class four students in my all male college had been pursued into the assembly hall in various shades of undress by a combined team of male teachers and prefects under the command of the principal. With some genitals dangling from side to side, with unwashed soap foams, unwashed buttocks and half-clad towels they have been herded into the assembly hall. It was to the glares and unsavory comments of other students and staff of the college. Their offence: coming late and not coming at all to the morning assembly. The disgrace was not enough for the principal who went ahead to clamp three weeks suspension on the students to the bargain.

I don't know or rather can't remember now how it all started but somehow a peaceful protest was organized to redress the indignity meted out to our classmates. It had been a peaceful protest until some bad boys took full charge of it. The first sign of trouble emerged when all the prefects were singularly rounded up and given a hiding of their lives after which they were locked in some of the school toilets. Before some order could be restored by some sane students, a section of the imposing administrative edifice of the college went up in flames. The police had arrived probably at the invitation of the harried principal.

I was in one of the unlucky batches of protesting students that were caught and taken into police custody. But it had been more of an adventure; the police used tear gas only in dispersing the rioters. In the cell, we were given a separate section which kept us away from hardened rogues and law breakers in detention. And I had come out within twenty-four hours, so did others except those identified as the ring leaders. Our release had been mainly due to the fact that we had been locked up with the son of a serving State Health Commissioner. So when the police DPO was informed of this and ordered to release the commissioner's son immediately, it had benefited us since it would have been unfair to release just one person. Young men with impressionable minds wouldn't have easily forgotten that kind of extreme discrimination. But more crucial to our fate was the fact that the commissioner was one of the rare Nijans that still treasured a certain degree of fairness in their dealings. If his son must go, then his classmates

19

should go too since they all took part in the demonstration. Ironically it was later discovered that it was the commissioner's son Egege that struck the match that ignited the fire in the Administration building.

Apart from this experience that took place years ago, I only came across the police and not even the State Security people, at two places. At the road either collecting bribes or confusing traffic; and whenever I went to interview their P.R.O. as a rookie in the journalism profession when I had covered the crime beat for the Moon Chronicle.

Having stuffed my briefcase as full of my papers and articles, as they could, they hounded me out of the office. It was at the gate that I recovered my full breath and came out of my shock.

"Wait, let me inform my publisher on the phone", I said to one of the two men flanking me on both sides.

"There is no need for that he will be duly informed". The one that looked like the leader of the operation replied in front.

"Am I being arrested for what?", I asked.

"You will be informed at the office", the leader who was walking ahead with the other agent and cupping a mobile phone replied.

"Which office?", I asked as the door of a wagon car started opening. Traffic outside was low. The Urban Times had its office in an up-scale residential district. Darkness was suddenly assuming an eerie personality around my soul. It was the dawn of realization. My instincts were already no longer free and so would my body be very soon.

"The State Security Service", the leader replied with a breath of impatience and annoyance signaling it was the last question I would be permitted to ask.

That night in the confines of the security service cell was something to remember. Before I was sent to the headquarters' cell around 2.00am the next day Sunday, I was first taken to a divisional holding cell. Never mind about being told why I was brought in at seeing their chief. The moment you are with the security service men you are no longer at liberty. In fact to them you become an animal. You are to be treated that way too.

Two: Welcome Mate

In that holding cell where I spent five hours, I was given enough lectures to last me a prison time by some of the veterans of the state repressive apparatus. You attain the rank of veteran when you have been in and out of the claws of state detention up to three good times. Some of the niceties they told or tutored me on were largely in the realm of theory. This was why I hardly set out to follow them step by step and not to apply the logic in them in seeking meaning and explanation to my incarceration. I was led and developed only resistance and the refusal instinct as the occasion demanded in the evaluation of my warped memory.

One of these veterans, Khana took an instant liking to me. It was his fifth brush with the service. He had spent about ten years of his life in the various cells of the state security for various reasons or so-called offences bordering on human rights and agitation for democracy. For a young man of about thirty as I guessed with the not too bright light of the cell interior, I wondered how many years he had spent out of these confines as a free man.

With roughened skin and the countenance of a man who had seen it all and had absorbed the heat and cold of almost it all, Khana went through life and imprisonment with a detached mind the way I imagined. It was not that activities around him no longer bothered him but he had set his mind on achieving a better society and now takes the pains and sorrows that come with this lofty aspiration as part of the dues one must pay to attain an enduring goal.

Khana can be likened to a devout Hindu who had transcended the three lesser goals in life. He had overgrown the pursuit of pleasure, success and even service to others.

23

These goals had not brought rest and comfort to Khana's idealist personality, hence he has come to the most important and basic goal in life, that of detachment. But unlike the Hindu who pursue detachment alone, Khana was combining the pursuit of detachment with that of community. In fact, his state of detachment was in order to realize his goal of community service. Therefore, though his life was punctuated with joys and sorrows, he passes beyond them. It is not withdrawal from life; it is geared towards freeing a person from the results of his efforts. Khana then strives to work to the best of his ability and to serve to the best of his ability. Failure does not deter him and success does not inflame his ego. They are pit falls and transient passageways to the ultimate goal.

Khana had read most of my articles in the newspapers and loved what I was doing no matter how infinitesimal I thought it was. Of course, he was allowed the privilege of newspapers; his frequent sojourns had created a funny bond of understanding between him and his tormentors. So, he was allowed certain things that other inmates would dream about but never got. Khana had educated me on the methods of the security agents and their skilled interrogators.

Those special breed of intelligence men that are schooled in pervasive psychology who are duty bound to find out something from you to incriminate you. Khana told of their various deceptive methods, their torture or what they called persuasion and it was through these methods that they get you using orthodox and unorthodox means to confess and sign a confession even if you are innocent. That there are just two types of inmates in the state security cells and that the group you belong to decides your fate and not whether you have done what you are accused of or not. After all, some people spend years in detention and transverse so many kangaroo courts and tribunals or even sentenced in some cases without actually

24

being informed of their sins as it were.

As a result, if you belong to the 'must be jailed group', well you are doomed, be sure to get at least a five year term; even if you are accused of killing the President and everybody knows that the President is not yet dead. But if you belong to the 'harass and intimidate group', you will be released even after a court had found you guilty. In fact, the harass and intimidate group is used by the government as a propaganda issue. Therefore you might be sent home after a week of arrest with the government issuing a bogus statement to the effect that in keeping with its human rights posture, you are being left free. On the other hand, your case might drag on in the tribunals for some time. The victims of the State Security Service, SSS, are usually tried by tribunals for a reason we shall soon discover. There is built-up public awareness of the trial and then the government moves in and says that as an act of mercy and in response to intercessions by respectable older citizens of the nation, the charges are being dropped.

Also, you might have been convicted and already serving the sentence but the general public is yearning for your freedom because you never did anything in the first place. The government may even create an opposing view among their stooges in the guise of an interest group that will insist you serve out your term. Then in the heat of such controversy, the government will release you or commute your sentence and then issue a verbose presidential statement. That due to popular demand, pressure and the responsiveness of the government to public opinion you are being let off the hook or your sentence is hereby commuted to so and so years.

The retired army general was used in this way to cleanse the dungeon of a government fast losing credibility. His death sentence was commuted to five years. Of course he had been tried in a kangaroo tribunal and was never given the real chance

25

to defend himself in the first place. The general had been implicated by government security personnel (may be pandering to some vested and powerful interests) in some kind of religious disturbances with ethnic proportions. He had been accused of arming his people – the Banas and organizing them to fight their neighbours.

The Banas are an ethnic and religious minority in the area they inhabit. They were subject to all forms of marginalization and discrimination both from the local and state authorities. In the so called ethnic cum religious war launched by the Banas, it was the Banas who were the aggrieved and not the aggressors. Now, the dilemma lies in the fact that given the situation of this people and the relative prominence of the retired General, what should be his course of action if his people beckon unto him for help? Is he to keep quiet even where it becomes obvious that a war of attrition and extermination or near magnitude is being launched against his people? What if he kept quiet, knowing the opponents were watching his every movement in an attempt to clip his wings, and the war plus corpses of his people are taken to his door steps? This looks like a dilemma we may not be able to resolve on the pages of this narrative.

On arrival that night around 9.30pm at the premises of the divisional SSS, I was immediately led to a punishment cell where there were already four other hapless citizens. The room that served as a holding cell was a little more than half the size of a normal room, which is a ten by eight feet room. With four sweating men already inside and only a pothole at the door for ventilation, it was stuffy and had the acrid smell of human sweat and waste. The four men were lying in sleeping positions and there was no further space for the next person, me. The four groggy eyed guests of the SSS blinked at me and continued their business. I had no option than to lie down and by sheer weight created a space for my seventy kilogramme size among the four prostrate bodies, each of us lying on our sides and each person's hip bones threatening that of the next man and vice versa.

But the SSS were not yet finished in their inventive and architectural display of human beings. Thirty minutes later, two other men were showed in; one obviously a priest going by his bedraggled and dirt sodden cassock. That was the end of sleep or whatever we were trying to achieve by closing heavy but painful eyes. Eyes rheumy and torn tatters by the inner humiliation of the soul and owl like privations of the body.

Everybody got up and sat on buttocks. Shirts, cassock and all were removed and stacked by the door as the room was by now suffocating and the grey bulb at the centre of the room was not helpful as it did not give enough light but emitted enough heat; we couldn't put it off as its switch was not inside the cell. With seven pairs of legs rubbing and shoulder blades touching each other we had a go at cell intimacy that nobody could have avoided. It was time for discussion and exchange of experiences. Our acquaintances were under way.

"What are you in for", the small sized but handsome Khana asked.

I shrugged non-commitally, as I can only try a guess. Maybe something I wrote in the newspapers or somebody had given me away. Throughout the ride from the Urban Times and till the present I had brooded over my likely offence. It was impossible to pinpoint what I wrote that sent me here. Journalists are often interred because of their pens and mine was a poignant stroke of reality. Two weeks ago, I had come out with a feature article entitled: "Watchers Never Win". It had been an article aimed at stirring the people into the realization of their plight. It had in part read:

...it is the people who allow destiny that is an intangible quality to rule them. To have a destiny is to chart a course of progress and development. To be ruled by destiny is to make sure that progress is always attainable and aspirations lofty. The moment Nijans realize that without their effort and concretized actions, the plum office of the nation's chief executive would continue to be a grab all affairs is now. A price that only the boldest and most callous in the land would get. Until the truth of collective damnation dawns on us all, we might not crawl out of these muddy waters of our time ... A people they say get the type of leaders they deserve. If what we have now is not what we want, then let us act to effect a change. If illegality and illegitimacy are veritable tools in the hands of our leaders, then let us use them in much more artistic and noble manner to free ourselves from this yoke. Like the goat told the palm tree, to stand aloof is to be cut down prematurely but to run, fight and bleat is to last longer. Until the battle frees us, Aluta Continua.

My publisher and Editor-in-Chief had called the article then a clarion call to battle; and patted my back. An anti-establishment sort, my publisher, a former newspaper editor who had met fortune was in league with any endeavour to topple any authority except his own. Maybe the above article was the source of my present discomfort but I had written what I consider greater and more poignant articles before even last week my article had urged Naijans to get ready for a cleansing revolution of some sort.

"I bet it's because of your articles in the paper, I guess you have stepped on the toes of big brother with your anti-establishment opinions", the irrepressible Khana continued.

Next in the questioning line was the clergy man who kept mute and after some persuasion, he blurted out in a deeply bored voice, "I'm not a common criminal. I love the church and my motherland". His face seemed subdued and reminded one of the visage of someone just waking from sleep but his corpulent skin and obviously high quality cassock though bedraggled and dirty testified to happier days. He must be about five feet six and had the habit of perpetually flexing his fingers and emitting those dreadful crunchy sounds from them. With slightly bright eyes and a large mouth struggling to hold down an over-full set of dentition, he must be something on the pulpit.

"We are also not petty criminals". I volunteered.

"If you are not, you are definitely enemies of the state and I'm not. So me and you people are not in the same category", the priest intoned with an air of finality.

"Talking of category", Khana quipped in, "nothing defines category better than sharing such a closed up space as this".

"May the good Lord forgive you", the priest answered in a confession box tone and turned his back to the rest of the crowd. He later became a little bit more receptive to other inmates. This was expected since the cell was a great leveler of people. Incidentally, the inmates took to calling the Pentecostal priest "Man of God" or MOG for short.

The man who came in with the man of God introduced himself as a manufacturer of some sort based in this city and also a landlord, probably of the common specie now – Sherlock. He guessed he was in cell because of a quarrel some days ago between his seven year old son and the son of one of his tenants of the same age. The landlord's son had given the frail looking but troublesome tenant's son a beating of his life. Both parents had been attracted by the Sunday afternoon howling of the boy, while the landlord tried to placate tenant and son; the tenant had thumped his chest and threatened brimstone. The tenant who gave out that he was a public servant with the Petroleum Ministry was in reality a low level state security operative. The landlord had been whisked off this evening by the tenant and some colleagues.

29

But point of fact, the SSS can be regarded as public service. Weren't they those in charge of critical elements of the nation's security? But their powers are immense and the present regime had given them more weight than imaginable. Whatever an SSS wanted, he did. They are virtually above the law and were also wielders of the law. But the downside was that the law and those they serve often turn on them. It was not entirely new for those in the know that SSS officers often disappear into thin air or are wasted in strange and often macabre accidents. Those who know too much among them often tread the thin line between life and death.

Other inmates were in the cell for one so called offence or the other. One of them, an associate of Khana, was a reticent huge man. The other, a young and sorrowful looking fellow, a student leader; while the last person was a known social critic whose rubicund visage and healthy skin gave a kind of lie to his status. In this country, social critics are supposed to be knickers wearing, agbada shunning, skinny and unkempt set of men who have adopted the corrupted appellation 'comrade' or any other self-assigned altruistic prefix. With proper dressing Bello Usman could pass for a CEO of one of the multinational firms in the country. But Usman's name rings a bell, both at home and abroad, where he had led as well as actively participated in various solidarity protests and marches for the sake of an egalitarian ordering of society. Nobody had told him yet that his ideals were utopian.

"What is your own offence?" I asked the student leader.

"Do the assholes tell you? But I guess it has to be for one student activism or the other. They want me to renounce protest and confrontations with the authorities as well as give them the names of other student leaders and collaborators". He paused, swallowed saliva and shook his head. At over six feet, with an imposing skull, a body a wrestler would covet and

30

ability to oscillate freely from one emotional state to another, he seemed an interesting handful.

"Are you going to do that?" I probed.

"No way, they are wasting their useless time. They have taken me to their headquarters; I have been interrogated and tortured there and then brought back here. But they are certainly wasting their lousy time".

"What of your studies?", I enquired, surprised at his courage.

"You see, we all progressives have to make sacrifices in our different ways to make this country better. You for example have been uprooted from your routine, from your family and friends, most of whom will not even know where you are now. What is your offence? Simple, if you don't know, you might have guessed, like Khana rightly pointed out. You have written something that does not agree with the neo-fascist repressive nature of this regime. By virtue of this attack on the government elites, you are clamped into cell under the superfluous assumption that you have committed a mortal sin against the motherland. But who are those who supposedly guard the motherland and arrogate to themselves the monopoly of deciding what is right or wrong for the motherland?"

The activist paused, surveyed his captive audience and continued:

"Bastards if you ask me. Like the leeches they are, they are there for what they can milk out of their so 'beloved' motherland. If they cannot settle or compromise you, they lock you up. For me, my education is important but not quite as important as the future of this great nation. As things stand now, my degree would hardly guarantee me a place in the nation and so would the future generations also face deep dilemma, so why not waste a little time and make things better

31

for us and posterity. I have gone through that choice in my mind for a long time and I'm totally convinced of the sagacity of my present course of action and I am willing to pay whatever price it demands".

The narrative of the activist captured the full attention of Khana who obviously has identified a kindred spirit and must rise up to the occasion. Khana stood up to his full height of five seven. Though not as tall as the activist, he was still imposing with blue penetrating eyes, hawkish mouth and a nose that seemed perfectly made for the face. His frame had achieved that fit between small and big and his hands were always in free flow motion whenever he was talking. Occasional stabbing of the air with the index finger precedes the making of important points or agreement with some other view. He was literally born to be restless, so pacing back and front became routine whenever he opened his mouth. He was indeed born for the rostrum.

"Like Mr. Okonkwo has said", Khana took over turning a little to the left in order to face me squarely, "the battle to save the country by progressives is already in motion and no amount of repressions and detentions will deter us. If we do not do it, who will do it? In my family while growing up I was brought up not to avoid responsibility. We all understand the pains we suffer and the anxiety we cause loved ones by our peculiar plight. But we are also convinced of the cause we are fighting for. We live in a society where the governor does not look beyond his nose and hence governs for his own interest and not the interest of the people he is supposed to govern. And no matter how difficult they make things for the common man, they still go about with toothy smiles and a retinue of overfed and misdirected men. They are stooges of neo-imperialism who have sacrificed their conscience and sense of duty on the altar of materialism. The country according to

32

dependable national and international projections and studies including some sponsored by my group have enough resources to ensure a healthy living for everybody till the eventual second coming of Christ. So why the mind-numbing and heart boggling poverty? Over 80% of our people live below the bread line, while a tiny percentage live like manorial lords. They are people whose lid of reasoning has been clogged by dews of want and selfish quests. They are yet to realize that they have torn out their spirits and thrown same to dogs in exchange for the flashy allures of a life that is bound to end at dagger point".

Khana paused, warming up to what looked like a favourite subject of his. "Look at Mr. Clergyman that is here with us now. He must have preached one indicting sermon today and promptly they dragged him cassock and all to a cell. People, even men of God can no longer say their minds. And every day we are harangued in the government press about the human rights posture of this regime. Who is fooling who?"

I took another look at my cell mates especially the fire spitting and oratorical ones with a renewed sense of respect. Prison was looking up as an abode of dignified personages. Their stoic calm to things was moving and more outstanding was their conviction and sense of altruism. Like Daniel at the lion's den, they have been dragged to a precipice but have refused to give up their convictions even at the risk of being pushed over. God knows the amount of fortitude I got from listening to them and hearing a stated commitment to such beliefs.

Apart from the student activist, the likeable Khana was very interesting. They say there are mainly two types of public speakers, those that can make you realize your circumstances only and those that can make you realize your circumstances and rise up immediately to do what you feel will assuage the injustice taking a cue from their speech. They won't urge you

33

to rampage or bluntly call you up to arms but whenever they finish speaking to you, something in the form of concrete action whether positive or negative slips out of your consciousness and directs your reaction to such a speech. Khana was of the second type.

Suddenly everybody in the cell including the wall communing priest agreed we wanted to ease ourselves. It was a ploy to get some fresh air outside since the half room was now very unbearable. So Khana banged on the oak door repeatedly until a sleepy eyed agent materialized from the darkness of the passage and in a gruffly voice demanded, 'what's the matter? We told him, rather Khana told him our desire, and he ordered us to wait and slipped into the darkness again. For the next twenty minutes nothing happened, Khana was about to start banging on the oak door again when a hefty AK47 wielding agent appeared from somewhere. Opening the door, he stepped to the left side and gesticulated to the right for us.

"Out, follow your left and hands behind your back. One false move and you are dead". The guard hollered.

But he shouldn't have worried; escape was very far from our minds that early morning. And there was hardly anywhere to run to or to hide in the country if the SSS are really after you.

Outside the poorly lit squalid courtyard of the hardly imposing but surely nondescript SSS building, a curious half circle of agents were formed. All with hands either in their trousers or suit pockets obviously romancing their revolvers. One thing can be said for these guys, they know how to keep their quarry in line. We were led to a plot of half green bush behind the building where we chose plot-lets to discharge our wastes. Surprisingly most of my cellmates went beyond taking fresh air and actually discharged faeces. I tried to follow suit

34

but couldn't, my bowels though willing, my mind was not in it. The scene was unsettling, what with the bush and the agents flashing torches on each squatted man ever so often to make sure nobody tried to scale the nearby wall.

I have always had this feeling that the act of defecation is psychological. Forgive my vulgarity but I feel defecating should be a combined enterprise between the bowels and the mind. That is why unless you have a bad stomach, you can defer your stool for even thirty-six hours, but you can hardly do the same with urine. Personally, I only do it when my mind is on it and my mind is usually on it only in the morning before I take a bath. And that cleansing state of mind during the morning ritual facilitates taking decisions on some crucial issues within that period of exercise. I have taken so many important decisions in that unholy position and I know of friends who have confessed to the same complex.

Secondly, I have always had this obsession with privacy. I hardly pull off my clothes unless the other party is naked and you should know in what position. I believe people's ability to cover their bodies especially the mid-region is a source of the immutable human dignity attributed to the higher animal, man, so I only pull off in the privacy of my bedroom or bathroom and not in front of cell mates and the searching eyes of uncouth and gun swinging security agents.

Again, the spectacle of the open plot turned toilet would be enough to gum up the bowels of any normal person. Although those in detention, as I found out from experience are hardly normal. The moment you enter detention you are reduced somehow. A light drizzle it seemed had fallen minutes before we came out, all available spaces in between the bushes were congested with various shapes of human faeces in various stages of decomposition, while the recent ones that have not been dried by the sun were given nauseating shapes by the

35

drizzle. They looked like the shape of an unplucked over-ripe pawpaw fruit that fell to splatters on a soft patch of ground. The fresh air we came out ostensibly to get was thus polluted. I don't remember now which one was better to the nostrils, the acrid body smells and air hanging in the stuffy cell or the putrid burst of night air outside.

"Your time is almost up, start cleaning your buttocks and pulling up your trousers!" the overbearing guard with the machine gun barked.

"Nobody dares hurry me when I'm easing myself. You can haul me in here with your devilish weapons but you dare not hurry me in this private affair". The priest retorted.

"You might well be using up your toilet time for the next two days this night if you don't take time".

"Give them five more minutes, Sammy. And go easy on that man of God".

A suit clad agent, one of those in a semi-circle said. He was obviously the most senior among them all on night duty.

A period of over five minutes passed and nobody including me who was not participating in the ritual got up to the exasperation of the agents.

"Hurry up, here you learn to do it quickly", the burly guard hollered again consulting his watch.

"You mean in this hell hole of yours?" the student activist asked.

"Yes, I mean in the security service as a whole. You waste little time and strive towards efficiency", the guard replied.

"In civil society people are never hurried out of the toilet", the vocal Khana answered getting up as he finished speaking. This was taken as a signal and every other person got up and pulled on their pants.

"You mean the security service is not a civilized society", the guard asked fuming.

"I don't think I will call any place where responsible and respectable people are waited upon with pistols and machine guns as they ease themselves in public that distinguished name", Khana replied with an air of superiority, leading the pack. We were marched back to the cell.

Around 2.00a.m., the burly guard came to call me. He informed me from the door that I was being taken to their headquarters. I bid my cell mates goodbye. In a touching scene that lasted less than two minutes they whispered some encouraging words in my ears. Khana had repeatedly said one thing, be strong and don't give up the cause; while the student activist urged me to take my mind off the immediate situation and put it on what the country will be if right triumphed. The clergy man only murmured a terse God guide you, and the landlord simply waved a lame looking hand. It was easy to discern why he was the most crushed of all. The others had sleepily murmured one thing or the other.

Three: Solitary

Solitary confinement. That was where I found myself early Sunday morning in the SSS headquarters. I guess they must have chloroformed me in the car from the divisional cell. Before I describe my new hovel for you I would tell you something else that is equally interesting. I woke up Sunday morning, I knew it was Sunday morning even though there was little light in the cell because most people would surely know when it is morning even without opening the eyes especially if have you cultivated the habit of waking up very early in the morning.

Also out in the country yard somewhere, prisoners or rather inmates (I'm led to use the words prisoner and inmate, cell and prison interchangeably because for me they all refer to basically the same thing. Actually some would go on to argue that the lot of the convicted prisoner is better) were welcoming the morning with various noises while their custodians marched up and down distributing chores and instilling fears into their spines. I was in my underpants only. They had neatly stripped me.

Apart from an aversion towards indecently exposing my skin, stripping somebody naked brings home to the person one other fact about his cell life. Like all other total institutions especially mental hospitals and sanatorium, the cell or prison is made primarily to strip somebody of all his previous personality and dignity. The mere act of stripping somebody naked, half naked, giving him a number and uniform as practised in mental and penal institutions aims at voiding their personality and de-sanitizing their inner most person; their subconscious mind. At the SSS headquarters like any prison set-up, people are not referred to by their names, this rarely

39

happens. You are given a number which now approximates you. You are like a new slate, a clean and new paper that is blank; it becomes the prerogative of the authorities to wield their fancy on the blank paper.

Submission to authority is also achieved this way. Inmates become lambs that obey their keeper without bleating. Like the man on the floor is subservient to the one on a chair, the inmates are totally inferior to their custodians. Your status before incarceration does not matter once you are in, because you are being turned into a new being that must grow like the guardian wants. When little flowers are plucked from the main bunch and family and planted elsewhere, the planter takes charge of pruning the flower, cutting and watering it as either the flower demands or as he the horticulturist desires; the flower does not make any vocal demand and does not object except by atropism. But are human beings flowers?

But unlike the planter of flower, the operatives here are supposed to operate within the framework of a laid down legal instrument. Yes, but the myth surrounding their service is that the laws of the land look as if not made for them. When a man is fully armed and given the power of life and death over other mortals, he becomes something else. The law becomes something to harken to if it will satisfy their whims and something to discard if it will inhibit their cruelty in any form. And the accused inmate and culprit have no voice to be heard. Not that you are not allowed to talk while in cell or shout your head off if you so wish. But none of the above vocal actions would in any way change or tinker with your predetermined fate in the hands of the SSS.

Right from day one you are made to fully appreciate the fact that you are alive because they are magnanimous with you, hence you become aware also of the fact that you are totally under their mercy. This creates a pseudo-complex of fear and subservience; you don't snivel or complain about whatever they wrought with you. You become like a toy in their powerful hands and you would be glad if the very inventive and imaginative ones among them don't turn you into an experimental animal.

When you witness what befalls others in the same place whatever small measure that is spared you becomes a thing of immense gratitude. If you witness others having their toe nail peeled with pincers because of one misdemeanor or the other and you are not eventually subjected to the same horrible experience you will then practically learn what it takes to be grateful. It is not a matter of courage because courage is when you have a choice. When all avenues are closed on you, then there is no question of courage arising. The only courage available is that form of courage that allows you the strength to go through the entire trauma without losing your bearing.

My solitary confinement cell was just a quarter or less the size of a small room. The type one is confronted with in highly urbanized commercial cities in the country. It was barely spacious enough to take a full grown man. There is no provision of a bed or bunk, I slept on a thread-bare blanket on the bare cement floor, and at other times I slept standing up. Impossible you would think but the old saying about necessity and invention have never been proven far from the truth. Like the popular Ghanaian musician sang, "landlord travel and see", so unless you go there you won't be able to imagine this. There was an old water closet tucked into the wall at one end, though the ration of three slices of bread laced with beans two times a day does not encourage bowel activity. There was nothing like supper or dinner, inmates are kept hungry after the afternoon meal of bread and beans till the following morning.

It was part of the physiological warfare to wear down the resistance of the inmate. A pot hole on the steel door provided

41

the only source of light and air as there was neither provision for a bulb nor a source of ventilation in the cell. Apart from the tiny hole on the door, the whole place was sealed and airtight. The steel door was in a passage with poor lighting.

If you have been in solitary confinement cell before you would fully appreciate my trauma. Confinement is a nerve racking experience. It is designed to greatly destabilize someone and drive him to the edge of his intellectual equilibrium. Those who have had prolonged stay there without learning the art of sleeping while standing have come out sad patients and some have died while in solitary. Little wonder it is the habitat of recalcitrant and troublesome inmates. A good visit to the confinement cell will certainly drive out the fight in most of the recalcitrant and stubborn ones. Being confined in a solitary cell confirmed my fears that they would probably hang a sedition charge on my poor neck. I was not afraid of that as I was sure my conscience was at peace.

There are cases when the conscience reasons otherwise and the body feels the other way round. In such a case the personality becomes disturbed as it is now compartmentalized into disagreeing sections. I was no longer interested in the issue of innocence as I have been told by Khana that what matters is what they want to do with me and not what I have done or not done. After all, the state does not incarcerate you most times on political grounds because of what you have done but because of what you are capable of doing or even what you have failed to do. Even individuals and firms (including newspaper houses) also punish people for not doing something rather than for doing something.

I vividly recall my experience in the Moon Chronicle while still a rookie in the business of feature writing. I had written a scathing article against the activities of the so called mafia that is supposed to determine the political and social dance tune of the nation. In the said article I had written among other things that:

...clandestine activities no matter how sedate the practitioners intended them never bring good but evil. The mere fact that a group of men and maybe women are doing business shrouded in secrecy and darkness is enough to cast long shadows of doubt and evil passion on their intentions. Those who we can refer to as the political Mafias in this country have neither denied their role in the unfolding political drama in Naija nor removed the huge masks over their faces, they have remained faceless. Even those who have gone a step further beyond conjectures and insinuations and have called the names of some people who belong to the mafia have had their insinuations and cat calls unreplied or at best have got mild rebuttal from those accused. The Nostra mafia might exist as a group of men and women in glamorous wears or austere habits who dream of arrogating all powers in this country to themselves but never attained this dream. So who is afraid of these toothless and crowd jittery brood of armchair and pedestrian reformers?

...It is time we see the Nostra Mafia for what it is, a group of misguided and misdirected people who now want to dance calypso with the fate of Naija. Let them sleep and roast in their sleep if they so desire but they are not in any way relevant to the geo-political entity called Naija.

This article was the start of my journey out of the paper. The chairman of the paper was deeply (unknown to me) engrossed with this amorphous group either as an active member or as one of their antennae. It was after my ouster that I found out that the mafia existed in real terms and was on its way to being effectively decisive in crucial matters in the country. The Moon Chronicle and a good number of other mass media channels were sources of realizing this ambition.

My offence had been an inability to praise the mafia or water down their callous nature on grounds of the notion of

43

the freedom of every Naijan to hold free associations and belong to mutual benefit social groups. I was convinced of this because a colleague then covering the social profile section of the Chronicle had often written on this mafia but usually in glowering terms and focusing on their bogus social lifestyles. But it was a different ball game when politics becomes involved. But my so-called colleague, one of the curious throw-ups of the muddy waters of journalism was a mole for the government. Quite a good number of such people can be located in any sensitive organization in the country. Their remit like that of the Gestapo informers is to sniff out opposition, severe criticism and hatred of the government and report sources of these to their pay masters in the State Security echelon. Sometimes innocent people end up behind bars and mesh wires because of snippets of conversation they had in taxis, buses and bus stops.

People, who are classified haters of the regime, are made to denounce some friends and relatives. This the security agents achieve through use of 'persuasion' on such people. Those that break – and this is a relatively large number – give names of innocent people while the few that persevere are hounded and hunted intermittently but never killed for their obstinacy. Those that give away friends deserve no blame because the agents usually believe that just like any negative sentiment against the government is shared so also any plot. As a result, catching one person alone does not suffice for them. Again, your ability to weather the storm of persuasion depends on your physical and emotional make up. But incarceration influences the personality often in radical ways. Thus, virile and emotionally stable men have been reduced to groveling and sobbing creatures by the experience of detention. While some naturally weak people have ended up with the most resilient personalities while in detention.

Your ability to remain unruffled and dare the SSS sometimes owes greatly to your anticipation of detention and its consequences. People who have gone through the route before or many times like Khana only give out what they want to give out and no more. Those who are exhorted to be resolute and determined before they are taken away sometimes make it if they keep a good hold on their minds. Exhortation outside the walls of the security service is a different kettle of fish from what accosts you inside the four walls. Those who were lucky to meet friendly people in cells and divisional cells before being moved (a holding cell can be any cell that is owned and maintained by the state i.e. the Police, Navy and Immigration cells anywhere in the country can serve as holding cells for the SSS) to the headquarters also face the same dilemma.

The first experience of detention might make their minds go warp, but if they survive the mental degradation of the first few hours then they may go through with little chances of breaking beyond their will. It is akin to cult initiations in college where your ability to survive the first night out and keep a good control on your instinct of fear determines whether you pass through all the other stages; but if you succumb to the instinct of fear, you give up and not appear for subsequent nighties. In the cell, the first few hours are not the worst but they are crucial to whatever might result from the other harsher treatment you would face especially during persuasion. Just like the composure of a candidate few minutes into an examination determines sometimes the eventual grade the candidate would make, the initial reaction to incarceration is often the most determining.

My mental state in seven days of confinement varied between determination and despair. In my moments of determination and resolution which predominated, I cast my

45

mind over issues and events I have encountered in life. Even my so called moments of despair were spent likewise. I reflect on moody thoughts when in despair. I tried to fully understand man, his motive on earth, his reasoning and various shades of justification and ideologies he has built around himself since the inception of life. My first day – a grey Sunday morning – started on a despairing note. I was pissed off because I had been drugged against my wish and stripped almost naked.

On a day which started groggily and numbly I reflected on the issue of good and evil in man. Going through the notions of evil and good I tended towards the conviction of the Russian novelist, Solzhenitsyn. Evil and good are somehow twins and largely go together. Therefore, a thin line separates good and evil. They are opposite sides of a silver coin. It is very easy to go from one to the other; consequently one can move swiftly from good to evil and vice versa. But unlike Solzhenitsyn I do not believe that evil arises out of justification or that once evil is justified or made the equivalent of ideology, the evil doer continues and others join in the fray.

Primarily every human being has the seeds of good and evil in him and has the regulating mechanism of the conscience in him. Therefore, bereft of justification and ideology, the evil doer does evil because of choice. Such a choice may derive from his abnormal mentality or improper reasoning and logic. Often times this sense of logic or illogic is structured by beliefs, especially religious ones. Devout Hinduists rarely do evil since they are taught that life on earth is like a giant wheel. Each soul or person lives a series of lives thus having total experience. They are taught to do good because if a person is helpful to other people in one life time, the same people in different bodies will return the kindness in a later life time.

Similarly somebody that does evil or is violent in one life time will be equally repaid in subsequent life time. But more

46

than anything, the Hindu religion preaches that one moves towards Nirvana or union with God only when he has lived out a good cycle of life times. Where one fails in this spiritual bid, he will continue to incarnate until he achieves Nirvana. It cautions against egotism and arrogance because a person that is a beggar in one life might come back in another cycle as a king and vice versa. So the paramount rule is to be helpful to all beings and work towards being good.

But all the same the onus of responsibility for good or evil lies squarely on the individual and not really on any mitigating conditions. A man might be sent by another to poison someone and he goes ahead to do it reasoning that the murder will be on the one that sent him. Justifiable but it is not true, the man who is given poison to give another has been given the choice of killing or saving a life. If he goes ahead to administer the poison, he has killed but he could have saved a life by not administering the poison. Whichever he chooses depends on his basic personality which is superior to any ideology cum justification. Experience like they have argued can turn a truly good man into a dyed-in-the wool evil doer, but the fact remains that the two – evil and good – are alternatives and whichever one is chosen becomes the bearing board of the person. As a result the seeds of good and evil are in all of us.

We manifest the one which suits our personality at any point in time and leave the other latent. Like Tolstoy postulated:

It is a commonly held and generally accepted delusion that every man can be totally called good or evil. That is, evil and good can be compartmentalized. Whereas some people are wholly good, others are wholly bad. But this is wrong; hence everyman cannot be qualified to be wholly kind, wicked, stupid, intelligent, strong, and enthusiastic and so on. People are by no way like that. Subsequently it can be said for a man that he is more stupid than wise; more kind than wicked or at any particular time shows kindness than wickedness. Human beings are like rivers; the water is one and the same in all rivers, but in some places the river becomes broad, in others narrow, in some places clear and in others muddy; flows swifter in some places and is still in other places, in some places cold and in others warm. It is the same with human beings, hence every man bears within him the seeds of every known virtue and vice in him and now shows one, now another and is sometimes unlike himself while still the same man.

But Tolstoy's thesis does not exhaust the issue completely as I see it. This is because Tolstoy assumes that everyman must have kindness and wickedness in him. The only distinction being the degree to which each quality is apparent, therefore a man that is said to be wicked might be displaying sixty percent wickedness and forty percent kindness or indifference. This complicates and compounds the issue. Every man bears the seeds of virtue or vice or good and evil in him but at every point in time he shows one or the other totally. For the first twenty years of his life, a man might be totally wicked and after that he becomes kind may be for the rest of his life or some years. The time spacing can be as minute as to be calculated in seconds and minutes. But no man displays profound kindness that is not totally kind at that point in time.

This does not mean the same thing as Plato's concept of goodness where he argues that goodness is an absolute characteristic, man is either good or he is not. I would buy the absolute term if only a time dimension is added to it. I might reframe the Plato argument to state that goodness is an absolute characteristic that dominates the life of a man at each point in time. And evil is the same absolute trait that has a time reference in its total domination of a man's life.

Talking about good and evil reminds me of an incident that occurred in my third year in the university. Having taken one more downward glide in my bumpy academic career I took a decision to be good to all beings. I had failed a class seminar due to the vindictiveness of one of the low profile Marxist (I wonder what their new garb is now that the old Soviet Union had tumbled like a rubber doll on a beach) lecturers in the university. I decided to calmly take my fate and not display bitterness or evil intentions in my relationship with other students. It was not up to fifteen days after the start of the new academic year before I broke that vow. The vow to be good lasted me only less than fifteen days.

In the university I was given to the practice of giving myself a good drink as often as the strings of my purse permitted. I appreciate spreading my legs and bathing my tonsils with reasonable volume of alcohol and in relative comfort. So nine days after the beginning of the new academic year, I was still loaded and was sampling the various beer brands dominating the country. As a matter of insurance I rarely drink alone on campus. I usually go on a binge with a friend who must possess one qualification – that of being unable to match me bottle for bottle in the booze business. It becomes the duty of the poor guy to regulate my drinking and to sober me up as well as to see me safely to the hostel if this becomes expedient.

On this day, the lot of companionship fell on Jawara, a course mate. Jawara was a short, fat and overtly amiable youth that loved to live life to the fullest, though his small head can accommodate no more than two bottles of lager.

We went to the Student Union Building (SUB) and chose comfortable chairs and a table for ourselves. It was a cool breezy evening. I sat as a matter of habit facing the door of the joint. While Jawara was still devouring his first bottle of beer I was on the dregs of my second. I was far from being drunk but was in enough alcohol induced joviality to engage Jawara in a lively conversation.

"Look Jawa I have told you to forget that Nkechi girl. She's no good, no match for you", I said, signaling the barman for another bottle of beer.

"Jerry man, you seem to have forgotten that I started off with that girl on your genuine advice, or do mean to say you were insincere to me when you gave Nkechi the pass mark?" Jawa answered in his favourite Western baritone drawl.

"But Jawa that was last session before I discovered she was an economic plotter. I mean eh, a lot of water has passed under her bridge".

"How do you mean. She only asked for something I promised her all this while", Jawa defended spiritedly.

"When shall it dawn on you that any girl that asks for a present promised her as a debt is nothing but a plotter", I argued.

"No way Jerry, I know plotters when I see them. I can smell them. I can smell them miles away and I usually erect amphibious barricades against such babes", Jawa pursued.

"Something then is definitely wrong with your nose if you cannot smell the economy plotter in Nkechi", I stuck to my guns.

"You are entitled to your opinion, Jerry. Nkechi is my babe and I reserve the right to take decisions on her", Jawa blurted, slightly annoyed.

'Em…em, Jawa I mean no harm", I flustered, "I only wish to state that there are subtle plotters and bold plotters. So you should beware of …" I caught my breath and stopped speaking.

For coming into the joint from the glass doors was one of the prettiest things I have seen in my over two years in the

50

campus. A tall fair girl that oozed arrogance and sex appeal in every step she took. She walked the board like a gazelle. This girl knew what she's got and showed it off ostensibly for her attire was a shiny slimy thing that protected the legally unexposable things in front and back. The frock clung to her lush body and half of her back was open. Her supple body, fine arms and carriage stirred warm erotic feelings in my loins and I stared agape at her as she sat down next table to ours. Arranging herself demurely on the furniture, she ordered an orange drink from the solicitously hovering barman. It was a classic temptation for me.

Despite Jawara's caution I plunged into the fray.

"Hello", I beamed with a mirthful face.

"Hi", she replied, smiling coyly.

"Look baby, it seems I have seen this face somewhere?"

"I wouldn't be sure. This face has always been on my neck", she answered wittily.

I smiled, "Let's forget the normal toast lines and elaborate manifestos. I would want to know the owner of this striking face?"

"I'm Rita and you are welcome", she replied eagerly offering a well-manicured hand. I accepted the handshake.

My mind warned me to thread softly. It was as if the girl was too encouraging. There was this fashion in campus then of girls either roasting or looking for someone to bath them in drinks, chops and babes going alone to the SUB, putting on the best of their coy attire in order to trap an unwary male. But the Rita before me was strikingly pretty. She was what a friend of mine called a dangerously beautiful and critically well-built chic. Also I felt that after two years in the academic social cocoon I could very well manage any girl's intrigues and tricks,

51

after all we set the rules and play the game in this part of the world. It turned out that Rita was resident in the exclusive Presidential female hostel on the northern fringes of the campus. It was almost a good kilometre from the SUB and judging from how cool and easy she walked in like one on a short stroll I could not help asking how she came.

"How do you manage the distance?" I asked trying to pique her.

"No hassles, most of the time one of my friends who is mobile does the service", she said casually.

I was about asking the sex or gender of the friend but felt it was none of my business. Again I felt she was putting on unnecessary airs. She was pretty but appears not exactly the regular sort of babe.

So talking, we drifted on from one issue to the other. I spent almost all the money I had that day on the girl that called herself Rita.

She gave me a date the next night at her hostel. When I reached the room the next night I saw her cuddled in the arms of a beefy looking fellow. She introduced him as her fiancé and told me she was greatly grateful for my company last night but as I can see she is having a private moment with the love of her life. With a cheeky good-night, she subtly banged the door in my face. I abandoned my new oath of goodness and swore to deal with her ruthlessly. It did not take me up to a week to square up accounts with her.

Let's forget what I did and didn't do to her. But the above suffices to convince you that every man can be good at one time and wicked the next minute. But meanness (a variation of wickedness) as the general rule guiding an organization can hardly survive or last without some form of justification and ideology woven around it.

This becomes necessary if it is an organization that recruits people, an organization like the secret service and secret police can hardly recruit members and win their allegiance without such justification and ideology. This is because every man has his inner regulator called the conscience; the conscience is the prime mover of every rational action a man takes. So to subdue the conscience, some justification must be found that would counter the conviction of the conscience and once this state is created in the person it becomes easier to lure him away from contrary deep conviction with the aid of material indulgence. Ideology itself is used purposely to fire the zeal of the person obeying orders and doing the dirty job as well as to protect the superiority of those giving the orders.

Four: In The Name Of Service

I n the secret service, duty to the nation becomes the principal root of justification. You are ordered to maim somebody, paralyze him or even kill him. Don't feel any qualms about it; after all you are doing it for the good of the nation. The man you are sent to arrest even when you know or suspect his innocence is first proclaimed an enemy of the state, a traitor, a vandal. Once this picture of the person is created, you can now hound and hunt him and give him all sorts of cruel treatment. It is no longer an evil that you are doing, at worst it is a necessary evil that must be done for the good of the nation and any evil that is done to arrive at good is no longer an evil. You are brainwashed into believing in the superfluous sanctity of your assignment, your superiors exhort you to put in your best in the service of the nation. People who lose their lives in the service are extolled as patriots, worthy of any honour in the land. It is you against the enemies of the state, and who are the enemies of the state?

They are painted as those dark and evil angels who question the existing order of things. Those who arrogate to themselves the monopoly of reasoning, those who find endless faults in every step the government takes.

Gradually the ideology is bred. That only those that resent the goodwill of the administration subvert. They are seen and painted as collaborators with international enemies. They are neo-fascist agents of imperialism who want to undermine the independence of the nation. A curious we-and-them ideology bordering on foreign powers intervention and internal cynicism is built. As an agent you are the guardian of the unity of this nation, the other members of the public look up to you to ensure that our government does not crumple.

Forget the vocal few; they are here for what they can get. Are they not being sponsored by foreign powers to destabilize the country? They are the minions of their foreign masters. The harder you work in ridding this country of such elements, the more you would have contributed to the corporate existence of the nation. Those that criticize your work speak from ignorance; they simply do not understand and cannot appreciate what you are doing for the fatherland (motherland). As a result, organized evil and individual callousness seeping from it are justified and eulogized.

Hence, ideology legitimizes whatever cruel fancy of the human spirit. People are not inherently bad or good but possess capabilities towards the two. Experience can make one bad or good, so also is someone's personal belief devoid of religious influence. But I would also consign this belief to the area of ideology; it is part of the justification gab. That was why the notorious German nationalist Hitler committed all forms of atrocities against other races especially the Jews and Russians without feeling any revulsion or stomach cramp for once. I used to read everything about Hitler I could lay my hands on even as a grown-up because I have a belief that the world failed to scientifically and critically analyze the personality of the so-called anti-Christ. I believe that the world would continue breeding Hitlers if a good study is not done on how to remold those with Hitler organs into proper and ordinary beings. Perhaps the menace which the so-called neo-Nazis constitute to civilised human beings in present Germany testifies to this.

Though my reading of Hitler was not based on a belief or my ability to perform whatever physiological and psychological experiment that is required for this enormous task of personality reformation, it was done out of curiosity i.e. the

56

need to find out more and also to give myself an intellectual edge over other exponents of the Hitler theme, the Second World war saga, and the Nazi debacle.

Even in my cold solitary cell environment, I still remembered vividly the important things I have read about Hitler.

A mosquito buzzing in my ear interrupted my chain of thought. There were so many well-bred mosquitoes in the cell that only the stubborn attract my attention. Those are the ones that neither refuse to suck the offered blood nor go away but must keep a steady drone at the ear. This led me into remembering a story about the ill-fated wedding between the ear and the mosquito. It was a folklore my maternal grandmother used to relate to us with much gusto. And at the age of innocence it was enough explanation for the perpetual enmity between the mosquito and the ear. The story has it that the mosquito being the male went to marry a pretty lady – the ear. On reaching the venue of the proposed marriage with his kinsmen who might include the cockroaches and the bugs, the ear asked them who the proposed bridegroom was. The mosquito proudly stepped out, dancing jauntily on his two tiny legs. The ear rolled over with laughter, when her mirth subsided, she asked the love crazed mosquito, 'as you are now, how much longer do you think you will live?' The mosquito having been publicly insulted went back with his kinsmen, maybe after the palm wine must have been drank. Enmity then ensued between the male mosquito and the female ear. The ear expected the mosquito to drop dead any second (and possibly didn't want a high mortality family) and the mosquito uses every opportunity since then to inform the ear that it is still well and alive.

Having borne witness to this once more, I channeled my thoughts to Hitler and the basis of justification of cruelty. The

57

ideologies that cement wickedness and obliterate goodness in an otherwise normal person.

Hitler's seed of cruelty was sown while he was still a youth. It was the period when his bad nature being recalcitrant as in some people tried to overshadow his good self by all types of logical justification. His half-brother, Alois, was caught in robbery and wrote home requesting for money to prevent his going to prison. Meanwhile, he did not ask Hitler for money because Hitler then had none but asked from parents and relatives. Hitler stalled the move by replying the letter on his own and without properly informing those whose assistance was being sought. He wrote to his half-brother, that to steal and be caught doing it shows that you don't even know how to do it well.

You might feel Hitler was reasoning from the moral point of view, hence he who commits an offence should be punished for it. Far from it, Hitler was not looking at morality but rather at the frailty of human nature in achieving set goals, he had nothing but contempt for this kind of failure. As a result, his quarrel was not with the act itself but the ineptness of Alois. All his life, Alois showed a fundamental ineptness in almost everything he did. So Hitler justified his neglect of a brother in trouble on the basis of his inability to do most things well.

To justify his wanton annihilation of Jews, Hitler webbed a yarn of conviction and legitimacy that ran thus:

"First, Jewry definitely describes a race not a religious community. The Jew never appears as a Jewish German, a Jewish Pole, or even a Jewish American but always as a German, a Polish or an American Jew. The Jew living in the midst of an alien people accepts nothing from them but their language. And as little as a German in France finds himself compelled to use the French language or the Italian language in Italy, or the Chinese in China, so little may a Jew living among us be called a

German. Even the Mosaic faith, great as its importance for the preservation of their race may be is not completely decisive in distinguishing a Jew from a non-Jew. There is scarcely a single race whose members belong so exclusively to a single religion. In general the Jew has preserved his race and character through inbreeding often within very close family relationship. And he has been more successful in this than most of the people among who he lives. Thus we are faced with the fact that there lives among us a non- German, alien race which does not and is not in a position to sacrifice its racial characteristics or to renounce the emotions, ideas, and aspirations peculiar to it, yet nevertheless possesses the same political privileges that we do. The emotions of the Jews remain purely materialistic and this is even truer of their ideas and aspirations. The dance before the Golden Calf has been transformed into a merciless struggle for precisely those possessions which we following our most innermost feelings scarcely regard as having the highest importance nor as the only ones worth striving for. The value of the individual is no longer measured on the basis of his character and the important services he renders the community but merely on the basis of the extent of his possessions and his money.

The heights reached by a nation are no longer measured by the sum of its morals, and spiritual powers, but according to its wealth of material goods. From these sentiments is derived the thinking and the striving for money, for the power that protects the Jews and permits them to be unscrupulous in the choice of means and pitiless in the pursuit of their aims. In the states ruled by aristocrats they fawn on the majesty of the princes who abuse them, turning them into leaches of their own people.

In the democracies they woo the favour of the masses and crawl before "the majesty of the people". But all they know about is the majesty of money. They corrupt the princess with Byzantine flattery. National pride, the vigour of a people are destroyed by their derision and the shameless inculcation of vice … their power is the power of money which in form of interest endlessly and effortlessly increases compelling the people to submit to this most dangerous yoke, so that they may learn that glittering gold becomes burdensome and has tragic consequences. All the highest things men strive for, religion or socialism or democracy are for the Jew only the means to an end and the end is to satisfy his greed for money and interest. The effect is to produce a race tuberculosis of the folk. (…) contemporary leaders are compelled in their own interest to accept Jewish support granted to them willingly and to deliver the goods demanded in exchange. And this return payment demands that they give every possible assistance to the Jews and above all prevents the betrayed people from fighting against the betrayers, thus paralyzing the anti-Semitic movement".

That was the conviction of the man a lot of people now see as anti-Christ for his ruthless genocide against the Jewish people. But he didn't end with the Jews; he also tried to overrun other races he could lay his hands on. Predictably, the black race did not merit the attention of Hitler as it does not exist. But if the Jews can be so branded and their punishment approved from the sense of perversion, what of the Russians, what sins did they commit against humanity in the all discerning mind of Adolf Hitler? Hear him on the justification for the destruction of Russia:

"While it is impossible for the Russians to shake off the yoke of the Jews by their own resources alone, it is equally impossible for the Jews to maintain that mighty empire forever. The Jews have no organizational ability but are a ferment of decomposition. The Russian empire in the East is ripe for collapse; and the end of the Jewish dominion of Russia will also be the end of Russia as a state. We have been chosen by fate to be witness of a catastrophe that will be the most powerful confirmation of the accuracy of the folk theory of race".

Hitler was edging to wipe out a race in order to prove the accuracy of a fancy theory which was the product of a warped mind. While he saw the Jews as selfish and with a highly monetized conscience, he saw the Russians as inferior and treated them with contempt and disdain. He saw the Russian soldiers as unfeeling (funny, wouldn't you say), full of half Asiatic stubbornness; poorer in intellect (and they were the first to visit the moon), weaker in will power (though they were the first nation willing to experiment with a nascent political system, communism); stronger only in the atavistic aspects of their useless lives. Hitler even justified his large scale deception of the German people. This was the only way he could drive them into doing evil against the rest of humanity. He knew the evil in his seeds. On the German people he used propaganda and averred thus;

"The receptivity of the great masses is extremely limited, their intelligence is small, their forgetfulness is enormous. Therefore all effective propaganda must be limited to a very few points and they should be used like slogans until the very last man in the audience is capable of understanding what is meant by this slogan. As soon as one sacrifices this basic principle and tries to show the facets of a problem the effect is filtered away, for the masses can neither digest nor retain the material offered to them. Thus the results are weakened and cancelled out altogether. The people in their overwhelming majority are so feminine in their nature that sober reasoning motivates their thoughts and behaviour far less than feeling and emotion. Their feelings are not complicated but very simple and complete. They do not have many varieties of shading, only love or hate, right or wrong, truth or lie never half of this and half of that or partially etc.".

But the above recollection on Hitler does not prove that somebody can be thoroughly bad by nature or wicked by nature. On the contrary as Hitler was bulldozing races based on noxious beliefs, part of his heart still harkened to the inherent kindness and softness in all beings. The same Hitler that roasted people alive and entered a war of genocide against other races, mourned ceaselessly over the suicide of a loved niece. This reminds me of a story I read in a book about the love crazed woman that drowned her illegitimate child because of her love for a new lover. The child was on their way so the young man told her to get rid of the kid and this she did by drowning the poor thing. At her trial, she pleaded guilty saying she did it for the love of the young man. Killing and loving at the same time, you see …

"Cell zero, your meal is here", some burly guard shouted from the grilled pot hole of my solitary cell.

When I turned to face him because I have been backing the door all the while, he dropped a crust of bread into my hands. Also about two cups of water in a plastic can was lowered down gently through a pulley string into the cell by the guard.

"Remember, you won't be getting another ration until eleven tomorrow morning". The guard announced disinterestedly.

"You mean you people got me in here to starve to death", I asked.

"Well I didn't get you here myself, for all I care you could have died resisting arrest. Mr. Newspaperman, you are in solitary and the meal you get is out of compassion".

"Thank you for being kind', I mocked, "What time is it anyway?" I asked.

"I wonder what you are going to do with it. It is ten minutes gone after six p.m. Listen let me tell you something, when you are here don't think about time or date because not knowing, you won't worry and whenever you are brought out you savour it and remain sane. Worry about the time and day and date, you might go off balance". The guard lectured gently staring at me through the grill.

Out of surprise I asked, "Why this sudden change of character? I thought you all are made of all stone and granite".

The guard didn't answer me but swore under his breath and marched stiffly off. I guess he must be upset. So I settled down to the crust of bread at hand.

****

That about gives all I do in my moments of despair. It would have been expected that I shed some tears (some people do), grovel or snivel during those periods. Nay, the macho in me put a stop to such open and sometimes superfluous expression of despair. Rather I looked at the world, the lives of great men and tried to give reasons to actions, and imbue notions behind acts that once appeared bizarre like those of Adolf Hitler.

But most of the time I spent in solitary, I did it with a firm resolution, a determination to live through the experience and come out stronger. With a renewed hope in the silver rays of life I gave my otherwise feeble soul a rock determination. My determination to outlive my persecutors stemmed from two reasons. My fellow victims with who I spent some hours in the holding cell have, while I was taking leave of them exhorted me to be strong. Some two hours before I was taken away, they had given me courage prior to the dramatic ones they displayed while I was leaving.

Khana had looked at me with beady eyes and said certain hushed words to the effect that the struggle was paramount. That I should not give in to charlatans and enemies of the progress of society. He had said finally; remember your ability to withstand whatever they give you and remain sane wins you their respect and our respect. But if you go there and grovel and snivel and crawl on your fours begging for mercy, you get nothing but their contempt. When you remain strong and concede only what you feel you have to concede, they respect your courage and take their time in dealing with you.

But when you plead and obey their whims like an over dependent dog, then they themselves will decide your destiny. Nobody will give you a written confession to sign if they are sure you are not going to sign it, but if you cry, plead and crawl before them, it means you will do whatever they ask of you in order to please them. The young student activist had also told me one thing two hours before my discharge from the holding cell; "I would like to read your article as soon as possible".

I would like to read your article as soon as possible. That was the parting words I received from the young activist. Later in cell, I came to realize the full import of this sentence and more than anything Khana said it kept me going. When the security operatives take you away their priority is not to make you go to the conventional cell. They may keep you under the pretense of interrogation with them for as long as they like and when they become satisfied, they will let you go. And it is on record that about three quarters of those that have gone through the grinders of the SSS in the country do not go back to the offence or professional calling that brought them as guests of the security service.

Why? The service aims at brainwashing people to tow the lines of the government; at intimidating and instilling life-long fears into them that they would now tread cautiously. The recalcitrant ones keep coming back and if they are not popular with the public, will meet with an accident while going to work or while at home or somehow. But die, they eventually must. Hence, while Khana was interested in my personal safety, in

64

my keeping the faith and coming out stronger, the student activist was interested in my remaining the same person on coming out and contributing my quota to the struggle by writing even more poignant newspaper articles.

But the thing that gave me the most determination was the family. I felt I owed them an obligation to return safe and sane to them. To pay back all the love they had shown me. I do not have what the white person would call a nuclear family of my own (the nuclear family of procreation) since I had not married and I'm not married even now as I write. But I have a more interesting family, the one that I came out from. I have my mother, my father, my step-mother and younger brothers and sisters plus a myriad of relatives – a long and winding nexus for that matter. In my cell my most sweet memories had to do with recollections of my life in the family bosom while growing up.

Father was not a polygamist by nature but succumbed to it later in life when I was already in the last year in the university and the other children were likewise out of the house in pursuit of higher education. All the same, we rallied to avert the disaster that threatened our family the moment a second wife was in. Everybody contributed his quota and the family became quasi-stable instead of totally disintegrated.

I vividly remember my first superfluous request in connection with schooling. It was while I was in elementary two at the age of six. I came home from school one Friday and announced to everybody at home that my best friend comes to school with a portfolio instead of a normal school bag. And that I wasn't going to school anymore until I was given one. Everybody including my father called it a joke and called my bluff.

In those days, the portfolio was very much in vogue and only well to do adult men carry them to and fro work. The only portfolio in our house at that time was the one my father himself was using. So my request then was at best a joke to them, but it was more like madness. But on Monday morning I refused to go to school, refused to eat and shunned all my playmates. I was in this hunger strike and moody frame until my father came home for break around 1.00p.m. By then school was over for the day. He called me into the parlour and sat me down.

"Now J boy, why didn't you go to school today?" J boy used to be my father's special sobriquet for me.

"Daddy, I want a portfolio", I answered stiffly.

Scratching his stubby jaw, my father spoke again,

"You know you are much too small and quite young for that. If we give you a portfolio now, what are we going to buy for you when you are in class six or when you make it to the university? It is not what you carry to school that matters but what you learn at school and you can only learn anything useful if you are not distracted by any outward show of pride and arrogance; moreover, you and the portfolio who would carry the other?"

"But daddy, UC comes to school with one and he manages to carry it, so I can carry mine", I argued childishly.

"UC's father is a commissioner; you know what a commissioner is?"

"Yes, somebody that follows the governor around always and is in charge of something". I answered, not grasping the logic he was laying.

"So you see, you are not UC, your father is not as wealthy as UC's and you may not be as strong as UC so as to be able to carry your own portfolio", he stressed reflectively.

"But em…eh but daddy you once said that you were UC's father's classmate. So if he is wealthy, you are also wealthy. After all our car is finer than theirs. Daddy you don't know that

66

I'm stronger than UC. We fought the other day at school and…

"You! What? Don't go around fighting at school, you heard me?"

"Yes daddy".

"Why don't we have an agreement", my dad proposed seeing I was not ready to budge.

"Anything you say, daddy".

"What was your position last term?"

"Third, I missed one class test".

"Alright, if you come first this term, you will have for yourself a new portfolio or the one I use now. Anyhow you prefer it, just come first". My father sounded firmly, getting up to go back to work.

"But daddy, you know…"

"Shut up. You will get a portfolio as I stated and not otherwise. Now run along and tell the driver to bring the car to the front". He ordered, dismissing me and ending the issue on his own note.

I went back to school the next morning and prayed to God to help me come first. I didn't put in any extra hours to improve but relied on God. At the end of the term I didn't come first, but there was a compromise, I came second. Since I came second I didn't demand for the portfolio but my dad felt otherwise. In his own logic, since I didn't come first I wouldn't get a new portfolio but a fairly used portfolio in view of making an improvement. So he bought a new one and bequeathed the old one to me. New or old, the portfolio made me the shining star of the school the following term.

UC had discarded his own out of a reason I couldn't fathom, though he told me it was too heavy and burdensome for him. I never believed an iota of that, because he dropped six places last term I felt that his father took the portfolio as a

67

result of that. Since he was a classmate of my dad, he would behave like my dad in similar circumstance, I reasoned. And because UC comes to school chauffer driven, I didn't believe a mite of the burdensome and heavy argument. But I found out this was the case within two weeks of the start of the new term. By the third week, I had discarded the portfolio and gone back to my old light and swinging raffia decorated school bag. But I was the star in my school for the few weeks I used the portfolio.

Five: Moments to Ponder

I t is really amazing how your mind can wander through time when you are locked up and denied freedom, perhaps it was the attempt of a usually active faculty to keep busy and be in good health. On this wee hour of the day, with other free souls having succumbed to the clutches of deserved sleep in their various homes, I leaned on the wall of my claustrophobic cell and let my mind play its game of reminiscence. It went back years again to my childhood and my experience with trying to be sporty like the other kids. Incidentally, I have never made it in sports. In the first instance most of the competiveness; ruggedness; rivalry and muscle flexing that go with most sport activities nauseate me. But I had grown up in a family where my father was an avid football follower, who could not afford to miss any live match event on television. He was so enamored of the game that he had sometimes travelled long distances to watch the national team play, bearing the hotel and transport expenses happily.

On some of these football jaunts my poor mother whose love of football was the opposite of her husband's had been dragged along against her wish. This was long before there was a second wife. But don't even think for one moment that she would expose herself to any form of crass subjugation here since we had long discovered that my father's punishment as it were for dragging her along is a tradeoff whereby while he goes to watch the match in the stadium, she either stays back in the hotel room watching her favourite home movies; doing some of her endless needle work or even shopping whenever the economy of the family could take it. Of course these activities were things that my father could hardly stomach, especially the needle work. He could not understand how my mother could become so proficient and dexterous in something that has no apparent economic value. For me, I had always believed, probably motivated by the countless number of woolen products created ceaselessly for all members of the family that the needle work and its outcomes were mother's way of showing her unbridled love for her family. But my father belongs to the old school believers in the dignity of labour. For people like him, this dignity is related squarely to the rewards of labour. Therefore one should not shy away from labour so long as the exercise brings some tangible and valuable rewards to the individual involved in it. I am sure my father would have seen those who believe that labour can be for labour sake and those that argue that it can be perceived with or without economic rewards as a process through which human beings objectify their existence as big jokers. Even the religious philosophy of labour as lying within the desires of the Almighty for his people would also sound hollow to my father without a mention of the rewards for such labour. His was the case of a firm and unshakeable belief in the dictum that 'a labourer is worth his wages'. Thus, without the wages, the labourer might as well be a fool engaged in some ill-advised mental or physical exercise.

My father's love for football came, not from today's craze for European leagues but through his own involvement with the game. He had played as both the captain and defensive sweeper (whatever that means) for his old town football club – the Owa Eight Pillars. His mates still regale us with his exploits on the field on the few occasions we had been privileged to spend Christmas together as a family in the village. So having a father like him meant that I had tried playing football at some point in my primary school days but that zealous but un-spirited attempt had been snuffed out quite early by a memorable injury during a class practice session.

That the injury occurred during a class football practice session irked and annoyed my father to no end. He still cannot fathom, much less stomach the fact that the son of a former popular village footballer like him who was once the most dreaded defender in the entire senatorial area of his community had not survived a mere football practice of small school children in grade four. It was not just right to him.

But for me, after the initial pains and anguish of the injury I could see the brighter side of things. At least it meant I was done with football and other physically rigorous games and had good reason to be. The accident had been freaky since it would not have happened to a more experienced or field wiser kid. So on that eventful day, given my limited talents and lack of spirit I had simply taken an offside position on the other team's side of the pitch. I was just idling between the eighteen yard and the penalty spot waiting for any slip ball that I could muster the courage to play into the net with all my strength and whatever determination I could energize. My carefully hatched strategy to only attack the slip balls was torpedoed when Martin, the class sport captain shouted my name and gave a good long range pass from our own eighteen to me deep in the opponents goal area. I had reacted I guess a bit late since the ball went beyond me and headed towards the goal mouth, a mere twelve metres away. In order to prove myself and avoid being the butt of the jokes that would certainly follow from the fact that the ball slipped through my legs, I gave a desperate chase thinking I could get there ahead of the smallish looking lad in the opponent's goal. It was a costly miscalculation as the smallish boy was far faster and packed a bodily impact like pint-sized dynamite.

So we had collided just six metres outside the goal line as I was later told since I had passed out on impact and only became conscious of my surroundings five minutes later in the school first aid room. From looking at my disheveled and dusty sport wears, I must have rolled a couple of times on the dusty field after the collision. The knee injury was bad enough to warrant a hospital visit and the invention of a defecating posture that spared the knees from bending in the process for some weeks. These were in addition to a full week absence from school and hospital visits with the regular examination and treatment of my injuries by medical personnel who I suspected were enjoying my pains and anguish as the knees were massaged; bent stiffly over and over again with each exercise eliciting a hyena like howl from me.

This was fortunately the end of anybody's dreams of lofty sport ambitions for me. I came back to school subdued but resolute in my resolve of "not again". Luckily the school authorities could recognize a sporting coward when they see one and so no one bothered with me on that score again though I took to the less strenuous playing of chess and scrabble which had been grudgingly classified as sport and games only the previous year by the District Education Board. While my father ceaselessly rued and denigrated my choice of such unedifying games, my mother stood stoutly behind me and made me realize over and over again that I could not have made a better choice. Little wonder my mother bought me my first scrabble set and gladly played a game with me now and then.

I also recollect the day I beat up my immediate younger sister and got four lifelong welts from my father's cane. My younger sister until her marriage some years back used to be the tomboyish type and had more than her fair share of sibling jealousy. I was always quarreling and fighting with her. Sometimes when I remember all the quarrels we had as youngsters I end up blaming my parents. This was because the two of us were born within a period of two years. As a result I didn't give her the gap that would have been normal i.e. two or three years interval. While growing up, before the age of nine she became taller than me, though I later overtook her.

My sister Ann was not the respectful blushful female while growing up, though she's changed now. She was tomboyish, wild and rude. One day at about the turn of my eleventh year, we had a quarrel over one trivial matter or the other and she came to me as was her practice. But on this fateful day, two things were not in her favour. The night before I had decided on going to bed that it was time the sibling rivalry as personified by her stopped. This was a source of personal derision and scorn for me among close friends. They had often wondered how come I could keep my head high amongst equals and classmates and then my younger sister would continue to be a source of misery to me. Second, there was nobody in the house that day; even the maid was out.

Normally there should have been somebody (in such a large house) to mediate in our internecine bickering and fights. But on this day of all days we were all alone on our own (can't remember where the rest of the family went). Ann lost a tooth in the confrontation and got some blotchy red marks for her bravery.

My father came home that night and called me. "You know what you have done? You have made your sister an unmarketable commodity".

"Daddy I'm sorry. But you should have asked what she did. I didn't mean to injure her…" I lost my nerves but somehow continued,

"Ann is something else. She is troublesome and she knows she is a girl but would always be fighting a boy…"

I tried to defend myself. Already I was remorseful for my act and everybody in the house kept looking at me like I was the devil's incarnate. Even my mother did not reply my

73

greetings when she came back from the market and my younger ones were keeping me at arm's length. All were evidences of undisguised hostility because of Ann.

"So you know a man should not fight a woman", my father echoed advancing towards me.

But not me, I made a hasty exit. But I didn't eventually escape punishment. He woke me up from sleep the next morning around 5.00a.m, with a handful of whips. Like a trapped animal I had taken my due punishment. Despite my mother's bangs on the door and my loud cries for mercy, my father didn't give up until he drew blood. That was the last time I fought with my sister and it was the last thorough beating I received from my old man.

The beating instead of repelling me from him brought me closer. Because I felt in spite of myself that I deserved the beating for the injury I inflicted on my sister. I had fought her with an animal rage and had intended to harm her right from the onset in order to boost my chauvinistic ego. But once I did the deed and the madness was over I realized myself and saw that it was devilish to go all the way with a sister, even with an outsider. The flogging thence was received by my soul as a sort of cleansing; if I had not been flogged, I would have been tormented by my conscience for a long time.

My memory of my family or growing up is not entirely on the bitter or quarrelsome side. No way, it was also thoroughly spiced with the sweet and juicy parts, though the experiences that were bitter seem to last longer in the memory. Good things after all hardly last. But I reflected also on the sweet and enjoyable tit-bits.

I remember the sweet stories we used to exchange as innocent kids. In my primary school days my favourite history story used to be that of king Amenhotep IV of Egypt. I relish the tale so much and used to tell it to my younger ones

74

whenever it was my turn to give a story.

I guess they got bored of it but my dramatic style of telling it and my myriad gesticulations kept them listening on each occasion. Even in cell especially in my moments of determination in solitary confinement I used to recite that story as told by our lively primary school teacher of those days. Each time I felt like going over the brink and need to reassure myself of my mental equilibrium and sanity, I recite it as I have always done during childhood to the admiration of my brothers and sisters.

Amenhotep IV was the Egyptian Pharaoh who is credited with discovering the belief in one God. Amenhotep came to the throne at the age of eleven already married since the Egyptians follow the eastern culture of marrying early. His wife was his sister named Neferiti. She was his sister. The Egyptian royalty is one of the traditional households in ancient history where the rule of incest taboo does not work.

As a boy Amenhootep loved all things in nature, he loved the birds that sing, the mountains that intimidate, the deserts that loom endlessly, the trees that sway and his fellow men. This was unlike other Pharaohs before him who loved splendour, victory at war and great architectural feats. He did not want to kill his fellow men in the defense of the large Egyptian empire; that was unacceptable to him. Amenhotep was the sober and immensely reflective genre of humanity. Therefore, he gave himself to great thoughts and came to the conclusion that precise order in nature attests to the fact that there must be only one God.

He did not honour the gods of his fathers like other Pharaohs before him and had what may be considered haughty contempt for their priests who used their revered positions in the society to amass wealth and power. Instead he believed there was only one God and dedicated himself to discovering this God.

Amenhotep IV as a nature-lover was amazed by the generosity of the sun which ripened the fruits, warmed bodies of men and birds, dried clothes, food and animals. To him the sun was the supreme manifestation or epitome of goodness in nature and antithesis of evil. Hence, he believed that the sun must be the handiwork of the one God and gave his own sun god the name "Aton' instead of 'Ra" or "Amn-Ra" which was the name of the sun god the Egyptians had long worshipped. Aton means "the heat which is the sun". However, he bluntly refused to have images made of this his sun god.

But he had a difficult task of making his subjects believe in his God especially in the prevailing atmosphere of polytheism. Unlike other Pharaohs, he refused to have himself worshipped or idolized by his subjects and attributed such reverences and obeisance to his one god. In compliance with his new belief in one God, he changed his name because the old name contained the name of the sun god worshipped by Egyptians, Amen-Ra. His new name became Ikhnaton which literally means, 'Aton is satisfied', that is the sun-god (Aton) is pleased. He decreed that the worship of old gods must cease and sought to erase the images of these gods especially on tombs and monuments.

Ikhnaton built a new capital for Egypt as the former one in Shebes had too many monuments and temples telling of many old gods. This new capital was named Akhenaton which means in effect "the horizon of Aton". He had wonderful tombs and chapels built and the walls of these edifices were adorned with his own hymns and songs of praise to the one god. His core belief was that his one God was a God of love and kindness, who created all things. As a result he saw all men, including non-Egyptians as the children of the omnipotent one God. Although Ikhnaton ultimately failed to convince his people to change or accept this new belief, he never gave up. Therefore, when the empire of Egypt was being attacked, he refused to soil his hands with blood by defending it. For him and in line with his new belief, religion and truth were more important than war and bloodshed. Incidentally, Ikhnaton died under thirty years of age; a man who had preached in vain to equally vain people. Later on, years after his demise the Egyptians gave him a third name, 'that criminal' to underscore the triumph of the mundane over the sophisticated pursuit of idealism. A

mark of humanity then and still now; a world where the pursuit of the
vain and mundane is dignified and even valorised.

That was his due for preaching the higher sphere of
humanity to a generation steeped in the lower atavistic instincts
of humanity. Even contemporary society is full of so many
Akhenaton's who hold certain divine principles or social and
sacred beliefs as well as profound convictions despite severe
tribulations. You can imagine the type of fortitude the courage
of such men gave me while in detention.

Then there was my first experience of a date with the
opposite sex. An event I would always remember with
amusement. She was a dark beauty with deep dimples and a
generous overdose of smile for everyone. By that time I was
thirteen and in form three while she was twelve and in form
one in a girls' residential secondary school. Funmi was a
neighbourhood kid, she followed my sister to the house one
day and I fell for her. I don't know if she really fell for me too.
Though that day her over generous smiles and dimples got me
thinking it was possible but I later discovered she had a smile
for everyone.

At the end of one of my most enjoyable holidays,
Funmi went back to school and with the two of us being junior
students in boarding schools couldn't afford the privilege of
writing each other although we promised to write. But before
the school reopened that period, our relationship had moved
to a higher level than visits and letters as I had the opportunity
to cuddle her and move my timid fingers over her body though
we didn't go all the way. Moreover we were both too young
and inexperienced to go beyond that. Funmi's chest then was
as flat as mine and her only visible claim to womanhood were
her earrings and dresses. But I still clung to her sweet smelling
body and moved unsure fingers and palms as I have watched

adults do it on the screen. Funmi was always neat and crisp though then an innocent small girl. And I believe it was my encounter with her that made me grow an aversion and deep contempt for all untidy, dirty or unkempt females. It might sound like no point at all, but I have met plenty men who don't give a damn or don't care.

The next holidays I didn't see Funmi and have neither seen nor heard of her again. But the story was that her father who then worked in a federal parastatal was transferred to one of the northern cities and his family went with him. A different type of uprooting you would say, but it served to kill my first genuine love. But I wrote a poem in memory of our separation. It was an attempt at that age to capture emotion on paper and it was one of my earliest attempts at poetry. The poem aptly entitled separation ran thus:

Here our way divides
Separation is enlisting us
For every nice thing there is
Always an adjournment
We may see again but
The pain is benumbing
Sharper than any knife
Thicker than any virgin forest
Strong as storm
Fiercer than any evil
Conjured by wild dreams and sorcery
Walks like a marauder
Sometimes an evil wind
That blows no one good
But is also the subtle saviour
That frees the mind from
Bondages of love

And tribulations of the emotion.

This piece of poetry hung in the room I shared with younger ones for the next two years. In fact I brought it down when I fell woefully in love again, though by this second time I had become both street and bed wise. But it was Funmi that first opened that chapter of my life. Even decades after, I thought about it in my cell with unbelievable lightness of mien.

Six: No Illusions

I, Jerry Oldoh had no illusions about the dangers of practicing investigative and ethical journalism in a country governed by steel helmets that would gladly shoot first and ask questions later. In fact, no serious and honest practitioner of the pen craft was; not with the khaki boys in charge of state affairs and even more instructive, not after the ordeal of the brilliant journalist, Hanson Momoh. The story of Momoh is now akin to Practical Journalism 101 or Introduction to High Risk Journalism for all journalists in the country. Hanson was one of the most brilliant and pen dazzling writers the country had ever produced. To a lot of people, Hanson was a later day version of the journalist turned founding father of the nation's Independence from the East of the country who legend has it that even the dreaded white men who invented education and had the amazing ability to speak with both the mouth and nose respected his ability to run circles round them in impeccable Queen's English. In fact, the sage was captured in many popular stories as the father of "ism" which is a testimony to his ability to produce high sounding words and to even manufacture English words comfounding the owners of the language themselves.

Hanson Momoh's ability was proven in the fact that he commanded the respect of his professional colleagues in a profession where cloak and dagger was mainstay. Therefore, a good number of media practitioners were of the view that had Hanson been from the U.S or any of the Western nations, he would have won the Pulitzer or any of the other revered awards for his penmanship and daring approach to journalism. However Momoh had been one of the foremost and most vitriolic critics of the military establishment. Since the advent of the military in governance, which he regularly captures as the misadventure of the military in governance or the adventure of the military in mis-governance in his articles; Momoh had devoted over eighty percent of his magazine space to critical write-ups and exposures of the military and the callousness and corruption which have underlined its rule. He was an ardent believer in the truism that the military had no place in the governance of any modern state and had even argued that the worst civilian government is far better than the best of the military in governance.

While very much conscious of the parasitical nature of the political class in the country and the odious malfeasance of corruption and horse trading which masquerades as politics Hanson was all the same a solid advocate of civil rule. Momoh was known by everyone who was someone or something in the country and by all readers of dailies and magazines and even by the throngs of citizens who engage in the every evening ritual of gathering in drinking joints and pay per view television viewing centers in the quest for both entertainment and the merciful forgetfulness often induced by a regular worship of the bottle or a pent-up passionate following of Western soccer leagues. In such places, diluted versions and washed-up elongations of the gospel according to Momoh are often recanted by those who assume the extra privilege of access to news and gossips in more dignified environs. In circumstance as above, Momoh had built a larger than life image and a near cult worship borne out of his skill with the pen and the unquenchable appetite for investigative journalism. He was in short, dare devil and took immense joy from what he did. A colleague of his once narrated to impressed national television viewers how it was Momoh who came to work before everybody and left long after every other person and yet was found in the office even on Sunday afternoons through

82

evenings chipping away at his key board or browsing through various books and volumes of literature.

The only addition to the above ritual was when he was engaged in news pursuit or investigation outside the office. According to this colleague, Momoh was very much a social loner and one who loves working alone, only using others as sampling boards for his ideas when necessary. In spite of working alone, he was always the first to show the rookie the ropes and to send mails and SMSs to new colleagues regarding their work in order to encourage them. Even though he cannot be described as an outgoing socialite or mixer he would always put up attendance or brief presence in social gatherings of colleagues and friends where he would only sip mineral water and satisfy the enzymes with bowl of vegetable salad or tuna fish. He was also prone to make unannounced entries into official ceremonies and even social events using his journalistic prerogative as invitation.

Momoh expectedly developed a love-hate relationship with the higher echelons of the military although the details of such relationship are hard to fathom. So it was not out of place to see him in a beneficial dinner or state house party of the military brass. The amazing thing was that after seeing him ostensibly hobnobbing and dinning with the military big wigs in the night, you are bound to read his article the next day hammering even harder against the military. His focus were mainly on the stupendous corruption and human rights abuses in the military led government and how the lives of the military upper echelon were as far away as possible from the lives of soldiers anywhere else in the world. He once did a popular story on how the bulging stomachs of the military were the outcome of daily night orgies of pepper soup drinking and avaricious consumption of beer.

There was something spiritual, one feels, about the proclivity of the uniformed men in the country to the combination of very spicy and hot entrails of the goat or cow and cold beer. It was a consumption pattern that Momoh had repeatedly seen as responsible for the misshapenness of the military brass and their most unmilitary physical posture. An idea that was not totally original in its broadest sense since the French social scientist, Jean-Francois Bayart who I read his work as part of a final year development politics course had such impressions of the African political class in general. In fact, I still own a paperback copy of Bayart's book entitled "The State in Africa: The Politics of the Belly", the cover of which is illustrated with a picture of some caricature soldiers in some grotesque shapes and predictably armed.

I was actually uncomfortable with the book at first since I saw it as one more illustration of the pejorative view of the African from yet another Western writer. But I have since grown to even see the sense of repulsion about a group of people intent on ruining their people that informed the ideas in the book. Even though one could make a case of over-generalization and 'othering' (whatever academics mean by this) against the book, it all the same captures some basic realities of the affliction of consumption and its ruinous effects on the state in most of Africa. But the Khaki boys were too busy with important matters to have read any Bayart and one wonders if their formal grooming in such hallowed establishments as the Royal Military Academy, Sandhurst UK bothered with exposing them to such mundane ideas as those of the Bayarts of this world.

But Hanson's articles dwelling on how the state was often run from beer parlour joints and life and death decisions taken in a perennial state of stupor was sooner than later corroborated by the stories of a crusading former police officer who described how the pepper soup joints and officers messes were fast becoming the hub of government business. According to the police officer, not only is the state run largely from the outcome of the regular evening conclaves in such places but the careers of military personnel and policemen are made or marred from such places regularly.

There was therefore no love lost between Hanson and the military in spite of public posturing to the contrary by the military. Things came finally asunder with the story of the cocaine triangle revealing how an international drug smuggler caught by the drug law enforcers in one of the nation's international airports was actually a courier for a top military brass and how the celebrated capture of the courier with a record quantity of cocaine had later attracted punishment rather than commendation for the vigilant officers who made the mistake of capturing him. The courier was reported to have been whisked away from the drug law enforcement agency processing cell to luxury and freedom in London at the behest of the military. This story which ran conspicuously as the headline of the magazine for the week was perhaps the last straw; the proverbial handshake between Momoh and the military had gone beyond the elbow.

So it was no big surprise to those in the know that a few months later, Hanson was blown to pieces by an improvised explosive device. It was much like the replication of the deadly Iraq and Afghanistan scenes at home. His demise was as senseless as it was bizarre, bloody and wicked. While his relatives picked pieces of burnt and misshapen flesh to bury, three stories of what had happened gained prominence although no one could say with certainty which was true. The stories are:

Story One: This story which may be titled "How not to Play Poker with the Military" told of how Hanson got what he deserved by trying to sell a story that the public should have consumed to the military big wigs. According to the rumour mill, Hanson had stumbled on a story supported by the evidence of some unknown witnesses that a serving minister and one of the most prominent faces of the administration had actually flunked his final examinations some twenty years ago at the military academy in India. The story was that the name of the minister now 'Al-Amin' was the outcome of a change from his original Amin. Al-Amin according to the rumour channels was the name of the military academy mate of the minister who had died of unknown causes in the last week of their sojourn in India after the rigourous final examinations. So while Al-Amin had passed the examination a dead man, Amin had not been so fortunate. But given the 'everything is possible' bureaucracy in the country, the difference between the two names was as negligible as it was unnoticeable. So Amin had smartly assumed the name of the unlucky Al-Amin and breezed his way through the ranks within two decades of post-academy training.

The minister definitely is a very shrewd and street wise officer with enough polish to pretend within distinguished circles and more than enough knuckle to excel in the crude military world of the country. Moreover, he is a key member of the kitchen cabinet of the cabal in power and is even seen in some quarters as the anointed successor to the present maximum ruler. However, this story in spite its street-level popularity could not check out and the so called witnesses and sources from which Hanson got the story remained as illusory as the rumours themselves. Predictably nobody had any idea about the source of the story and when or to whom Hanson tried to sell the story.

Story Two: This story had more sympathy among discerning observers in the country since its broad outlines seem consistent with the *Modus Operandi* of the military. This "Dead before Speech" story simply told that Hanson was killed in order to prevent him from revealing what he found out about the maximum ruler in the country and his close pals. The problem with this story was that it could not point out any cogent or tangible issue or what it was that Hanson was prevented from revealing. It was more like allowing you to use your imagination and knowledge of the environment to fill the blanks.

This situation of things was not entirely out of place in the country where fear often does not allow people to clearly name certain things but rather give the listener enough hints to enable him arrive at the target conclusion. In fact, the use of slangs and euphemism in discussing current affairs and state matters had become common in popular culture. It was simply a safe way out of trouble. One can never tell who is listening or who your listener will talk to after you. Actually, it was common to end the narration of a juicy piece of story especially focusing on the social life and political misadventure of the rulers with, "do not say I told you".

I recall one of our delivery van drivers in the office telling me over coffee break one bleak rainy day about how his seven year old primary 2 daughter had told him the story of the school sport teacher who wore a torn trouser to the school one day and was prancing in front of the children taking them through a routine shoulder loosening exercise. This was in spite of the fact that his jean trouser had a gash in the front on the laps. The little girl ended the story to the father with the word, "papa do not say I told you ooh". The driver, Mr. Zubis was thoroughly disconcerted by what he saw as a very ingenious use of the clique by one so small. As for the torn trouser, Zubis told me it was one of those fashion things the young and young at heart go for since the teacher in question had simply gone to school with the so-called crazy jean that young people nowadays favour over the normal everyday jean. However, he still wondered why the teacher had not changed into a more appropriate sport wear before coming to take the kids in sports. Apparently he wanted to show off his fashion sense to the young ones and other teachers in the sport arena. Poor thing.

Story Three: I suspect that this story which could be entitled, "Greed and Partners" must have emanated from the rulers and their cronies. It was a story clearly supported by the government; and its media organs gave vent to it alas with subterfuge. It simply narrated that Hanson had fallen victim to one of the oldest predilections of humanity – greed. It tied the story to what has become an amazing success story; the growth of the print media establishment founded by Hanson and a few of his colleagues. The organization had grown beyond even the most optimistic expectations and was gradually becoming a gold mine in media entrepreneurship in the country. It was amazing how a semi-social detacher with no previous business experience could build such a successful business organization. Many people in explaining this often choose the easy way out by pointing at the fact that the flag ship magazine published by the organization should be expected to have a big market value given the strength of Hanson's pen and those of his other colleagues who are also accomplished writers albeit not as courageous as Momoh. But anybody with the slightest idea of business would know that merely packing a magazine with fine articles every other week does not just translate into healthy balance sheet and profits for the publishers. Quite a good number of media entrepreneurs have discovered too late that there is more to the cultivation of cocoyams than just bringing them out. Without doubt, the quality of the paper matters but a lot more goes into turning out a profit from a media organization with other secondary concerns than simply publishing good articles.

Also operating in an environment in which over sixty percent of the people are poor and could not be one bit bothered about such elitist concern as regular subscription to a news magazine raises the stake on survival. After all, the number of media organizations that have died in the country is about thrice the number that has survived. In fact, the media cemetery in the country is littered equally by outfits with quality articles and those without. For me, one explanation for the success lies in the dogged determination and commitment to work and sound business ethics by the whole management team of the organization. Anyway, back to our story number three. The idea is that the organization has grown so big and prosperous that some of the members of the management team had become very greedy and over ambitious. The development of this greed and untoward ambition had not been helped by the hands-on leadership approach of Hanson which these other management staff saw as simply micro-management.

To spice up matters, the story added that these other members were also not happy with the fact that in spite of the fact that the organization was started by the team together, Hanson had stolen the limelight and was the cynosure of the public eyes as well as the soul of the organization. So these dissatisfied members were cast as having become so fed up and greedy as to have taken matters into their own hands by hiring sophisticated killers to deal with the Hanson problem once and for all. This story as incredulous as it sounded was replayed in various camouflaged forms by the state media and got an official stamp of sorts when the press secretary to the Head of State infamously attributed the demise of Hanson to the unpredictable outcome of capitalist pursuit by professionals who know next to nothing about surviving in such environments where money was the only thing that attracts loyalty. Asked to explain himself by the journalists in attendance at this hasty media briefing, the rotund media officer, also a former journalist simply said, "read between the lines, gentlemen of the press". As one of the journalists present later narrated to his editor over the phone while filing the story, it was the irony that in a nation with an acknowledged over-abundance of human resources only the misfits hold sway in the corridors of government.

Unlike the Levites of old who were admonished from receiving any sacrifice with defects for Yahweh and not to consecrate anybody with defects as priest, the country got the injunction to make sure that only those with moral defects hold sway in government and its corridors. The editor, a part-time Pentecostal preacher laughed at this analogy and could not imagine anything more apt in this situation. Four years before his sudden meteoric rise to the position of press secretary, the man who now functioned as one of the most important official mouthpieces of the government had almost lost his professional accreditation and recognition as a result of disciplinary proceedings in a case of receiving bribes in order to suppress a public interest story. He was accused of having stopped the publication of the investigative report of the secret trading in babies in one of the very popular and large private hospitals in one of the cities in the North of the country while in office as the acting editor of the Northern Horizon.

This report which was written by an intern in the newspaper was accompanied by clear photographs of the perpetrators of the heinous crime and names of some interviewed witnesses. The now very important press secretary had simply used the evidence in the report to extort money from the medical director of the hospital and his partners in

90

the crime rumoured to be some of the very influential figures in the society. The hospital had simply exploited the increasing incidence of teenage pregnancies and fractious family relations which are either the direct product of the situation or the eventual outcome in most cases. It lures such girls into its facilities, feeds them well, promises them heaven on earth and nurse them to deliver the babies who are promptly taken away from them and sold to those in need of babies. The group never pried into what the buyers had in mind as goal for the purchase so long as they are willing to pay the dear cost and can be trusted to keep mum afterwards. The report if the now press secretary had published it would have made it possible for a swift public action to arrest the ugly development. Rather, the immoral syndicate operated for another two years before the law finally caught up with it.

Anyway, the fact that the Hanson media establishment had become a very successful enterprise made the story of greed and its outcome attractive to some sections of the population. However, the media stories immediately after the death of Hanson focusing on the sophistication of the plan and even the tool used in executing the plan suggested otherwise. One of the fragments of the device used had a serial number which some experts allege could only have come from an armoury since it is not sold in the open market and this was not Iraq, Pakistan or Afghanistan where all sorts of weapons bazaar functioned.

For me, I did not believe any of the rubbish stories bandied about rather gleefully by the government and its agents against Hanson. I knew deep inside me that he had unfortunately paid the dearest price for his fearless journalism and anti-corruption crusade. Fighting corruption in this land was like hitting your head against a strong concrete wall – you never leave any mark except your own blood and you never make any impact except on your own forehead. It was an entrenched and freely reproducing evil which has gone beyond being institutionalized but is now a norm and as sociologists would make us believe, norms are the definitional and predictable characteristics of the society. So our society here has corruption as one of its definitional characteristics. It was a pity it consumed such a fine intellectual and humane person as Hanson. He was one of the most down to earth and simple persons I have ever met.

I still vividly recall my first chance encounter with him. It was at a union of journalists meeting which I attended during the formative stages of my career. I had actually gone there at the behest of my editor then who felt my presence at the Newpaper's editorial board meeting that same evening might torpedo his aim to use the weekly editorial comments to massage the ego of one of the corrupt city administrators who was a lawn tennis playing mate of his and probably godfather to one of his brood of seven male children. So I grudgingly went to the union meeting even though I should have relished going since it was supposedly a professional association to which I belonged. Incidentally only those in the twilight of their careers and with political ambition or clout or worried about what would happen to their pension and retirement benefits made a point of attendance.

The only exceptions is for those who operated on the fringe of the profession and needed the cover offered by such gatherings to launder their images and of course those like Hanson who took bold risks in attacking the government and saw the solidarity of the union as something one can cash on in times of trouble. The meeting was rowdy towards the end as usual. I had been largely absent-minded throughout the proceedings, engrossed predictably in aiming imaginary bullets and arrows at the oily robust image of my unethical editor who had engineered my coming here by insisting that I also do a small piece for the page three top corner of the newspaper on the meeting. Apart from the lengthy discussion regarding the burial and social rights of a dead former colleague from the Eastern Times I could barely recall any other proceedings of the almost three hours long meeting. I was jolted out of my vindictive reverie by the loud clangs of the provost's bell calling for order and for members to move a motion for adjournment of the meeting.

This was received as good news since I could see people already gathering their stuff and stretching lazily in their seats in the manner only those about to be freed from a monotonous but necessary task and could not wait to do something more exciting do. Without surprise almost half of those present in the hall raised their hands for the motion, indicating everybody's tiredness and wish to dash off. The motion having duly been passed and the meeting adjourned, I gathered my papers and headed out wondering about the nature of story I was going to write about the meeting. However, I was not unduly alarmed since one can always web the stories around the agenda of the meeting which had been circulated the week before. The agenda only changed on two main scores from year to year: obituary and the president's speech. Just outside the door of the hall which opens out into the reception area of the three star hotel where the meeting took place, a gentle man spotting a white outfit hailed me by name and came bearing an enchanting toothpaste advert smile and introduced himself:

"Hey, I am Momoh. Hanson Momoh". Over-surprised because the name rang an immediate bell, I stuttered, "I, I am am………."

"Oh, don't bother I know you alright and anybody who cares for the future of this noble profession ought to take note of such an impressive young Turk like you".

I did a double take and exhaled, "I am glad you feel so sir".

93

"Please drop the sir, just Hanson will do. I am not one for officialdom, formality or primitive gerontological subjugation which is really laughable among colleagues like us".

I was totally in shock having just then realized I was having a discussion with the legendary Hanson. It was my first and incidentally last one-on-one with him. I surveyed the ordinary looking though dark handsome man in front of me. He was far handsomer and relaxed looking than the usual pensive looking and slightly frowning visage one encounters in the media photos of the man. The man before me wore a faded blue jeans, white polo shirt and dark lace-on converse shoes and clutched some papers now folded neatly and stowed in the left groove of the armpit. He was too simple to be true. As if oblivious of my gaping, and now that I know better, in a bid to rescue me from my fluster, he beamed a huge smile again.

"I like your writings and I hope to see you in our magazine one of these days. I just hope and pray that you keep faith and not fall into the abyss of greed and obscene lure of money that have derailed so many young talents in this country of ours".

"Thank you sir…I mean Hanson, I will do my best".

"I believe you will and I hope to see more of you. Actually you could give me a call one of these days. We can do a lot together for the good of this country", he said as he dropped his card into my open palms and moved off.

It was amazing. Such simplicity and candour. Anyway he met his demise a few months later and though I saw him again from a distance I regrettably never kept that appointment.

Seven: Simple as Style

I again ran into Hanson Momoh not quite two months after the press council meeting. It was at the annual media week celebrations in the highbrow Heavens-Bay Hotel where he was the key note speaker. As I now assume was his style, he appeared simply attired if not underdressed. He was clad in a pair of blue jeans trouser and a white polo shirt topped off by a matching blue cap. His dressing was as opposite as possible from those of the others at the high table in the banquet hall of the hotel, the venue of the annual media lecture which is the usual highlight of the five day long annual media week. The other invited guests and media union big wigs were either over-dressed in glossy and over-starched traditional get-ups (mainly of the kaftan variety) or they like the Honourable Minister of Information, the special guest of honour were clad in tight fitting Western blazers and suits. As if to accentuate the contradiction, the minister was seated just between Momoh and the avaricious looking union President who had ascended the office through the massive bribing of the regional delegates at the triennial conference of the union two years previously. As was widely rumoured then and as later events showed he was the government's choice for the job.

It stands to reason that in a country under a massive dictatorship the control of the media is always a big government project. In any case, the union president, apart from his football supporters' middle was a former features editor of a regional newspaper in the North of the country. Therefore Ahmed Imam's ascension into the enviable office of the President of the media union in the country was something of a big surprise. Not that there was any restrictions by the union's constitution on the rank or age of those who could aspire to the office; rather it was an office that the electoral process, because of a three tier level of voting favours mainly either well-known and experienced media practitioners or those like Hanson who have become household names through their penmanship. The election usually starts from one being elected a state delegate in the state he is based; from the state there is then the regional election of delegates (the country is split into four regions – North, South, West and East for this purpose) where each region elects six representatives for the national executive council. It is from those elected into the national executive council that a President is chosen by these delegates at the triennial conference. But the rise of Imam is only a surprise to those who are either unfamiliar with his romance with the military or those who see most things as innocuous. But as for me, I saw it coming, or how else would one explain the fact that when the country's main dictator embarked on a lesser hajj to Mecca, Imam was the only journalist from outside the government owned media in the media entourage. Then of course, the main thing Imam's pen has done in the last couple of years has been to justify the acts of the government with his now boring reference to dictatorial regimes in Latin America.

In his own understanding the home grown dictators were God sent people engaged in a difficult messianic exercise to liberate the country and even though they have made swift and strong decisions now and then they are still angels compared to what obtains in Latin America. One often wonders about Imam's linkage to the so-called dictators of Latin America. Anyway, the military lackey Imam was today clad in a flowing sky blue over-starched and over-ironed bubariga (a floor clinging and large size three piece kaftan peculiar to the Northern elites); while the minister did a poor job of enclosing his considerably big belly in a tight fitting dark red blazers protesting undoubtedly at the seams. In between them and clad in a simple blue jeans and polo shirt, Momoh resembled a very poor relative and perhaps out of place. Given the known inability of those in power in this country to articulate anything besides massive financial misappropriation schemes and cloak and dagger power schemes, the minister's speech lasted a very long ten minutes and was followed by splattering applause in which those on the high table (with the exception of Momoh and two other bored and pain looking media big wigs) led by Imam and the security detail of the minister stationed by the side door near the rostrum tried to outdo each other. This was in spite of the fact that out of the over two thousand people seated in the hall only a handful bothered to clap.

The charade of hand clapping soon died down and Hanson Momoh was called to take the floor and present his speech. The mere mention of his name more or less electrified the hall and he was clapped and cheered all the way to the lectern. It must be mentioned that the invitation of Momoh to give this address did not come easy or natural to Imam and his backers. It was one of those things you could not escape and given the somewhat ironic theme chosen for the year's media week, "Conscience and Duty in Media Practice", there had been a flood of international pressure and push for Momoh to be made the speaker given his outstanding crusade in these areas in the media in the last few years. In Imam's short-circuitous brain, the invitation of Momoh would give credence to his often repeated public protestation of playing by the rules and engaging the government only in the interest of the profession.

Imam is a staunch member of the ever growing school of thought that the only way to reform the government is to get involved and then reform it from within. Incidentally history has shown that those who get in end up being reformed by the government and not the other way round. I expected that the speech of Momoh would be punchy and insightful and I was not disappointed. While Imam in his opening remarks in his presidential speech had called on media practitioners to engage the government and stop being 'rampantly critical' (whatever that means) and anti-regime in orientation since everybody owes it as a duty to ensure the survival and growth of the country, in spite of whether you like those in government or not.

It was more or less an address shrouded in rationalizing the actions of the government once more since the sense of duty being foisted on the media by Imam has not been exhibited one bit by the government. In fact, any survival and growth in the country have been the survival of those in government and their cronies and the growth of their stomachs from excessive consumption. Anyway, Momoh characteristically chose to pursue the issue of conscience in his own speech. Although it has been some time now, I still recall some of the salient points made by Momoh. He first saw conscience as not just the ability of one to live without regrets with his actions but more importantly the ability to remove self and parochial interest in one's practice of public duty.

He was of the view that the media being the fourth realm was also a watch dog of public life and thus media practitioners should ideally see their work as public duty. To this end, they owe it as a duty to ensure that the public interest dominates all they do in their professional life. For him, duty then is guided by conscience and the performance of duty should be predicated on truth, courage and doggedness in the pursuit of the public good. In fact, he went on and on in an address that lasted over fifty minutes.

As would be expected the minister became more and more uncomfortable as Momoh went on with his speech drawing inferences of lack of duty and conscience from acts that even though carefully camouflaged as postulations were rehash of some of the actions of the government and its key actors. I remember a colleague from the Independent Day newspaper who sat by my side that day in the middle row of the hall turning to me after about twenty minutes into the Momoh address to hushly confide, "this guy is looking for trouble big time". I turned and looked at his face and could see how aghast it was. It was as if he was already seeing terrible things happening to Momoh right there and then. So in order to allay his fears and save everybody the risk of an uncalled hospital emergency since veins were popping up on his face, I answered, "old boy relax, all these things are just words. After all, he has written worse things in his articles and nothing happened to him. It's even good it is said here rather than writing them in the papers". This was unexpectedly helpful as my neighbor relaxed, took a deep breath and said, "I think you are right. Anyway, what is my own self? These big people know how to take care of themselves". Who said there is no God? Anyway Momoh ended his speech by calling on media practitioners not to see the week as only a week of celebration but also a time for sober reflection and rededication to duty. In his now familiar ending, he intoned, the mark of a good media is that it makes positive change inevitable by confronting bad leadership, corruption and mis-governance.

Momoh's end was drowned in a reverberating applause and a good number of the people in the hall including the formerly bored and pained media big wigs seating at the high table stood up to do this. I could not help but notice that while the union President chose that moment in history to search frantically for something missing from the bulky file before him on the table; the minister was engaged in a long drawn conversation with his aide de camp standing behind him. I could have sworn that both activities were contrived to avoid joining in the clapping and to create the pretense of not being fully aware of what was happening. Incidentally, Momoh left the occasion unannounced a few minutes after his speech and so those of us who had plans of shaking a famous hand and possibly thinking that by so doing some of his brilliance and courage would rub off somehow on us were denied the privilege.

I smiled mirthlessly, stretched my hands and rubbed my back on the wall of the cell to sooth the discomfort of one of the small rashes that had invaded my body since my sojourn here. Still thinking about Momoh I felt now as always that, it was a big pity the country had sacrificed such a brain on the altar of corruption, greed and insatiable quest for power. What a waste, it's still a big puzzle why the good ones never last. Someone, I think one of my catechism teachers said it was God's way of ensuring that they do not become bad. So he calls them home to Heaven quite early while giving more time to the evil ones to repent. But surely, God would have realized what's up now. The evil ones just keep on living and committing more heinous evils and hardly change their ways. The lesson was surely lost on the evil doers. Interestingly, these days liberal moralists and even some who worship at the altar of decadent philosophy would ask what is really evil and argue unbelievably that evil is just the act of society labeling those who are courageous enough to challenge it. It is that bad now.

****

By a change in the shade of light in the passage I knew it was getting darker outside. Soon enough the heavy crunch-crunch boots of a guard assailed my thought process. The crunchy boots stopped in front of my solitary and the guard peered in squinting thick lashed eyes.

"Cell zero, do you need anything?"

"I could do with some soap", I answered. The water in the toilet closet was functioning so I could rub myself clean but I hadn't used soap for over seventy-two hours.

"I will get you one although it is not allowed and some bread if you feel like eating", he answered without a change of features.

This guard had been keeping watch over my section since I came in there. He comes in the morning and does not leave until night when another guard takes over from him. The night guard was a mean son of a bitch who disturbs the peace of the night with the ceaseless crunch of his boots and torchlight that he beams into the cells every now and then. May be the night guard was paid to make sure people in our section of the establishment do not get any good night sleep.

The day guard was more humane and I wondered what got him into the service in the first place. He was responsible for bringing in a sleeping cot for me and clean beddings to go with it. A solitary detainee was supposed to sleep on the bare floor, the toilet seat or to doze standing up. But after forty-eight hours in the solitary cell and mastering the act of sleeping standing and leaning on a wall, the day guard had given me a cot. Whether it was orders from above or an inspired act of kindness I didn't know. He was certainly favourably disposed towards me. Imagine bringing soap and bread all of which were against their so called regulations. In solitary confinement you are denied most things and fed only once or twice a day.

One cold morning, the good natured guard came to my hovel and informed me it was a Friday morning and that I would be getting out of solitary over the weekend. I asked him, where I would be going from solitary. He said to the normal detention cell down the corridor. He told me there were two types of normal cell, the small cell and the big cell. The small cell contains about eight to ten people, while the big cell can take as much as forty detainees.

But that I shouldn't worry, he reassured, it's likely I would be taken to a small cell. There were some few spaces left in it and that I have behaved well so far even though I haven't confessed anything yet. When the guard left I had this euphoric feeling I usually felt as a kid when I have just been bought a new toy. I still wondered why this sudden change in policy towards me. I have been preparing my mind and body for another ordeal of torture and interrogation by the so called intelligence officers. A misnomer in names given that the principal weapons of such interrogations were beating and physical torture. Already I have been through one interrogation but was made to understand that by the going standard that it was more of child's play and a chat than an interrogation.

The said first interrogation was in a wide and long empty room like an ancient disco hall looking squarer than rectangular. The hue was white with no windows or space for ventilation. It was cooled probably by an air conditioner tucked away somewhere. The only furniture in the big room was a solid oak table and six chairs of similar kin. Sheets of paper were scattered randomly on the table. Sitting at the table were six men who could have passed for statues except that their mouths were moving, more mechanically like a set trap shutter than naturally. At the center of the table were two military men. One who incidentally was the chairman of whatever committee they formed in the large hollow room was a colonel in the military police going from his uniform while his colleague wore the insignia of a captain. A little distanced (as if maintaining the gap between the starched khaki uniform and lesser mortals) and sitting two from each flank of the military brass were four equally stolid and granite faced fellows in mufti. I guessed they

102

were from the security service or other such organizations.

I was pushed in roughly by two burly guards and the door to the room closed with a dull click.

"Sit down", a rasping voice commanded.

I looked around to see if there was any seat concealed anywhere in the large room,

"Sit down on the floor and don't waste our time". The same rasping voice. It was the military colonel.

I obeyed.

"Do you wish to make any voluntary statements, clarifications and comments to the effect that you have been undermining the corporate existence of this country? Calling on the people to rampage, aiding treason, and holding clandestine meetings and belonging to various underground groups aimed at furthering the above three callous and unpatriotic ambitions?"

The captain read out in a cackling voice.

It was like a Kangaroo court trial for a known enemy of the state and people. I was prepared for whatever intrigue their depraved faculties might swing but the magnitude of the above charges blew my mind. It fazed me somehow.

"Jerry, we are waiting for your comments. It is our belief that an enlightened man like you would talk with no persuasion to equally superior officers like us".

The voice was like a record playing on an old pin. The room was bathed in light like the stage of a Hollywood fashion film photographer. The goggles looked well-appointed and useful in the setting.

"Do you know I'm a newspaper man?", I asked meekly.

I was sitting yoga style on a tiled floor while my tormentors were on the high table.

The sitting arrangement like the solitary confinement was part of the on-going psychological attempt to wear down any resistance left. Once you sit on the floor, it conveys a message that you are the inferior being, more so nothing is as leveling as having to look up in order to see somebody's face. In the same vein, nothing is as ego boosting as looking down at somebody's head from a vantage position. Sitting down on the bare floor takes a normal tune when everybody else is in the same position like some socio-religious practices encourage.

"We know you are a newspaper man and other things as well", the old record player said.

"Then why do you think seriously that a responsible journalist and citizen like me would touch what you have accused me of with a ten feet pole?" I queried.

"We have seen gentler and more respected journalists plus handsomer fellows in the same game. So make your comments". The colonel said, sounding grossly impatient.

His constant look at his strap watch conveyed the impression that he was not ready for this assignment. In fact all of them had the looks of those going through a routine and would like to be over with it as soon as possible.

"I have no comments", I announced bracing myself for the worst.

"I must make it clear to you that you give us no choice than pushing you to our subordinates who certainly would get the needed information and comments from you with some persuasion". One whining voice from the mufti-clad foursome warned.

"I have not done anything wrong except to write my articles. I still believe I have a right to work in order to earn a livelihood in this country. I do not belong to any association except the Rotary Club. I don't see why you want me to agree to your concocted notions of me. Em… em I don't know what you are talking about", I fumed from a wrath I never knew was buried inside me.

Sanity would have cautioned against such outbursts from me in front of six armed men who obviously called the shots in a dungeon in which I was a guest. It was like daring a lion in his den and challenging one's god to a funeral dance.

The colonel lost colour and shot up from his seat like a thunderbolt. Waving a sheet of paper before me, he boomed:

"We have everything here. The title of your write-ups and the exhortations thereof are enough proof of your plans. It was my belief that you would make this part of the business as less dirty as possible by reading this and signing it. But it seems useless to give it to you to even peruse since you are intent at playing the saint with us. It looks like you are still strong and very resolute, but we shall see. You are going to sign this or you may leave here head first, period".

While the tirade lasted, I fervently mouthed a silent prayer that the colonel shouldn't become more dramatic. You never know, a bullet could fly. They were on a routine assignment and I have gained the first advantage. If you succeed in driving your opponent in any game to exasperation, then you are clearly ahead. So next thing is to brace up for a more determined onslaught from him at the resumption of hostilities.

But as I contemplated this, I wondered if I could survive the ordeal of the so called persuasion in the hands of subordinate officers. It was one thing to dare the lion and entirely another to stand your ground when it comes roaring out to take up the challenge.

Less than fifty seconds after the outburst from the colonel, the two burly guards that brought me came and roughly took me outside. This convinced me that closed circuit monitoring was in use in the building.

The guards took me to another room though smaller down one dark corridor. There I was beaten to pulp with freshly cut thick sticks. I howled and cried out, but never begged for their mercy. I lost consciousness and recovered in my solitary cell. It was strenuous and painful standing up. I looked thoroughly at my body; all bones were intact though there were bruises and welts all over my body especially the back and stomach. My face was in one blotted piece, it was the work of experts. To soften up and not damage the ware. I was feeling hungry, sore and like somebody ran over by a lorry.

I was having one helluva time in detention but I wouldn't sign a confession of things I had never imagined in my life.

I was happy at the prospect of leaving the solitary even though I have almost fallen into a routine in it. But nothing has ever threatened my sanity and bearing than the confinement. I was going to a normal cell where I would see and hear normal people who were suffering the same persecution. And on a general note I was going to a place where I would get better treatment than the solitary provided, a place I would exchange and share experiences with other hapless citizens.

It was on this euphoric feeling that my memory riveted once more to my family and the fun of growing up. I remembered clearly what mother would be doing this morning that is if she hadn't heard of my predicament. If she had she might be battling high blood pressure in one clinic or the other. But on ordinary days and times, mother always wakes up early and gets busy from then till night fall. She is the hard-working type, sometimes I used to wonder how she keeps going despite all odds.

But I have long given up wondering as she had remained a source of encouragement and challenge to other members of the family. These days when I meet ladies with a pretension to being homely, I snicker inside because I know that they can neither compare nor compete with my mother on that score. Invariably I always end up using my mother as a measuring instrument on other ladies I meet. And they usually fall short, far short. Maybe that is why I have not got married.

Old fashioned you may say but a man's mother most times invariably becomes his model of a woman, a mother, a wife and even a girlfriend. A man craves to see the good qualities in his mother replicated in any woman coming to share his life. And nothing irritates girls nowadays more than a man that uses his mother as a measure of all things good in a woman.

Sometimes you don't blame them. After all no two beings are exactly the same. Short of sounding chauvinistic I think their irritation derives from the point that they know, they stand miles short of the ideal woman. If not, what is wrong with a man desiring what he feels is the ultimate especially in relationships destined to last long, like marriages.

But the modern women as they are now called deserve some concession from us, what they cannot make up in the core area of domesticity and disposition they try to make up in their nascent quest for professionalism. Hence they are faced with too many pressures and demands in the modern world they only try to do their best. They are generally trying in this endeavour. But the older generation of women mostly had demands and pressures that were within the frontiers of their homes. Their worries were mainly limited to the periphery of their domestic fronts.

I remembered the last conversation I had with my mother on the issue she said was bothering her greatly; the issue of my getting married.

The conversation had taken place about six months ago when I went back to them during the Christmas period. I had a four day casual leave and traveled East to my family. Luckily for me, they had not yet left Aba for the village for Xmas and weren't going home that year for the yuletide.

One morning, that was on my second day at home, my

mother called me into her room and sat me down.

"My son, I know you don't like discussing what I want us to talk about but I feel I must still discuss it with you", she began on a plaintive note.

"Mother I have told you before that you can discuss anything with me despite what you feel my reaction would be", I reassured her.

"Eh… how is your newspaper work? I heard you write very well these days".

"It's alright; I'm just doing my best". I said non-committally; still to get the drift of her thoughts.

"I heard also that you write so many bad things about the government", she said, making it sound more like a question than a statement.

"I write what I see. What are the truth and the real situation of things? It's not my fault if the government has only a few good things one can write about", I answered getting impatient.

"Do your superiors in the office appreciate your work? Please don't allow anybody to mislead you or use you as a pawn".

"Don't fear about that. Whatever I do is what I want to do. And meanwhile you are being wrongly informed. I write facts but not condemnation of those in authority", I answered believing myself then.

I have never counted myself among the social crusaders or among the growing number of self-proclaimed social critics.

"I hope so. You know your father does not have much support for that newspaper job you are doing". She cautioned.

"Whatever father likes is his business and whatever I like is my own business', I answered, getting slightly irritated, 'but mother I hope you didn't call me this early morning to chat about my job'. I enquired.

108

"That and another thing, my son".

The irrepressible mother of me. I knew that something more important to her was in the offing; the first issue about my job was just the opener. Like the use of a pawn in an opening move by an expert in chess. For my mother, the first thing discussed is used to loosen your mind, keep you in suspense and anticipative of the second and main issue. Also it is a gimmick used to dismantle your guards if you have built some. So that the main issue would find you flustering, helpless and hence give the true and candid answers and opinions demanded. Cunning woman.

"Have you finally found a partner?" she asked

"You mean in my office?" I pretended not to understand her drift.

"You know very well what I mean. When your father was at your present age, we had already gotten three children including you". She pursued.

"I must say you people were fast". I still tried to sound funny.

"Enough of the wise cracks, Jerry. When are you getting married?"

"As soon as I find a woman I like". I answered as I have always done.

"Do you mean to say, you are yet to find a woman you like with all these girls milling all over the place?"

"Maybe I don't want the milling specie".

"Maybe it's time I look for a wife for you on my own", she offered the panacea she had always offered.

I declined as usual, "unless you are getting her for yourself. I will find my own wife when it is time".

"Which time are you talking about? Is it when you grow

grey hairs that you would know it is time to marry?" she attacked furiously.

"If it comes to that, I wouldn't be the first to marry with grey hair on the head". I countered.

It was not as if I didn't respect her opinions, far from it. But I have gotten sick and tired of everybody in the family reminding me of how long expired my bachelorhood was. I don't know if I am anti-marriage but it has definitely not been on my agenda in life. I have experienced women though sparingly and only when I need to reaffirm my manhood. Right from my entry into the male-female sex relationship I have not been able to have or make a relationship last more than six months. It has always been a drift in, drift out affair with women.

To reassure my mother and not ruin her Christmas, I answered her reflectively.

"I'm going out with one girl now. She comes from this part of the land, if things work out well it wouldn't be long before we tie the knots".

That was enough to lift the gloom on her face that morning,

"I hope you finally do it this year. Your father is as worried as I am. Soon tongues would start wagging if you are normal at all".

But it was a bland lie on my own part. I was not moving out with anybody that period. The last female walked out of my life in October, but assuaging my mother's feeling even through lying was more important.

You might be wondering about my father. In a nutshell he is the domestic authoritarian chieftain with a large overdose of democratic pretensions. My old man is a master of the game of domination. It is always his heart's desire to have full autocratic control of everything related to him, from his pair of slippers to his wives. Maybe it was his wish to reassert his authority and get my mother in line that led him to the throes of polygyny; though I have come to look at our polygynous family as more of a blessing than a curse. For my father, the old adage one ship, one captain, should be the universal axiom of all family units. Hence, he believes without overstressing it that everybody should succumb to his authority and tow his lines. You only use your initiative when he has nothing to offer in that quiet and controlled demeanor of his. But he has definite but sometimes contradicting pretensions to democracy.

Before he makes any crucial decision, he calls those concerned and makes genuine effort to hear their views on the issue. But the funny thing is that he has already made up his mind and despite your opinions, at the end of the day his own wish becomes his and the family's command. No matter the battle cry, it must emanate from him. I learnt him quite early in life, anytime you feel he has bought your opinion, it is only luck that was on your side. It simply means that you and father think the same way on that issue. Maybe he uses this democratic pretensions to foster love in the family and more especially engender love from all members of the family, because one would have found it difficult to truly cherish and purely love a father that rules his household with such a tight-fisted but understated iron claw.

But his belief aside, he is a gentle and loving father who believes that his children should not lack the basic necessities, but abhors luxury amongst the young as this leads to their peril. His attitude to luxurious living often borders on some puritanical orientation like that of the famed Calvinists of old.

All the same, my old man has that bit of a tyrant in most

men, hence any disobedience of his order is seen by him as an act of treason. The rebel is seen as the shame of the family. In my own way I am a rebel and so are other brothers and sisters who dared take an independent decision on any serious issue. My land marking rebellion was committed the time I was choosing a course of study in my last year in secondary school. I had been good in both arts and sciences in school, that my old man felt I should end up in one of the so called professional disciplines like medicine, law, engineering, pharmacy etc. but I had my own idea and would have gotten away with it but not easily with my father still in the picture. One cool evening, he called me into the parlour and questioned me.

"What would you like to be in future?" he asked in his usual deep voice.

"You mean profession?" I asked

"Of course".

"I would want to be a journalist", I answered with all the pride I could muster.

"A... what?" he asked astonished. Then in a lower tone;

"Why do you want to be a journalist of all the things in this world?"

I couldn't answer him frankly as I would have loved to do. I was afraid of his reaction and I was already confused by his outburst. It had been my ambition to be a journalist for some time. The source of that ambition was not farfetched.

I drew it from a practicing journalist and from my English language teacher in secondary school. How would I tell him that Mr. Roberts, an English language teacher in my school had totally influenced my choice of profession. Mr. Roberts, the eloquent and awe inspiring teacher and orator, who for two good years was my idol of worship had one day confessed in class that the only thing he regretted in his life was his inability to become a journalist. Why he didn't become one, he didn't tell. If Mr. Roberts who I saw as an embodiment of all good things could crave for the pen wielding profession, then I was bought. Another pillar of influence and encouragement was the veteran journalist, Felix Adewun a.k.a. Feature-Felix. Right from the first moment I started making meaning out of scripted newspaper articles; Mr. Adewun's write-ups were incisive and gripping. Feature-Felix as he was called could pass as the best feature writer the country has ever produced. Even today when I look through my scrap book of articles, I still feel that Adewun was the Lance Morrow of Africa.

Eight: War Stories

While I sought to achieve the dream of Mr. Roberts, I also craved to surpass the classical achievements of Mr. Adewun.

"Dad, it's what I want to be', I maintained my stand.

"Look young man, journalism is a fine profession but it is not the place for you'.

'Why?'

"Sometimes it is risky especially in this country now; moreover it does not pay as much as other professions. Who wants to be a newspaper man, while others make the money you report in your tabloid how they make the money and how they spend it and so on'. He argued with a habitual sneer.

"Dad, it is not the money that matters to me, but the job and the name'.

"Which kind of name does a journalist make for himself in this country? He who reports on the activities of some prominent people and those people he reports, who is greater? The town crier can never be greater than the king. And you better know it; money is the universal determinant of events and destinies in this century".

"May be I should not go to school at all, and then I can pursue money like many others without much education'.

'I don't mean to say money is everything and I hope you don't read me like that. But at least you need to be comfortable, own a car, a house, put your children through good schools, and eat whatever you and your family desire. Are you not going to have a family? Do you ever imagine how much it costs a week to feed you all in this house?'

He was not finished yet.

"And if the son is going to be greater than the father as our

115

people pray, I expect you should take care of your family on much grander scale'.

"Dad, you are impossible. Don't journalists eat, don't they have families? Are they beggars? I know there are some who are not doing well but some are well off. It depends on how well you do the job". I tried to argue.

"I have said all there is to it. You are my first son, I expect you to listen to me now, but when you become a man and own your own house, you can take decisions independently". He said with finality and left.

You see what I mean by tagging him the domestic dictator with democratic pretensions. Well, I went ahead to read journalism to his great displeasure. Though we did not become anyhow estranged, he has not totally forgotten or forgiven that early show of independence on my part. And anytime the younger ones show obstinacy he invariably brings it all to bear on the first family rebel – me.

In spite of the above flashes of domestic dictatorship, my father is still one of those remarkable characters and heads of house hold that are in charge without being too loud or pushy; at least before late age polygyny pushed him into snapping and shouting at the least provocation. But by this time, we were all already out of the house or in the university. An ordinary observer of our family while we were still growing up would readily see my mother, with her daily sermons (reprimanding talks and warnings), strutting about and emitting verbal threats on her children as the one who calls the shots in our house. But this was not so as my father quietly maintained his authority and commanded the respect of his wife and respect mixed with fear from us. However, in spite of his normal serious orientation to life and ostensibly snobbish posture, my father was in certain things a passionate person. But if there is any other passion I can ascribe to my father besides his ardent love of football, it is his passionate retelling of the stories of the Biafra civil war. Apart from stressing his own bravado during the war, his only other take on that 30 month civil war was that the collapse of the breakaway Republic of Biafra is the greatest misfortune that had befallen the country.

So while others would preach unity and re-echo the sentiments of the victors in the war that "united we stand" or "the nation's unity is superior to any other sectional, individual or group interests", my father believes that all the current social and political problems in the country can be related to the collapse of that rebellion. So whether you complain about epileptic energy supply; autocratic regimes; economic recession; or even youth unemployment my father had just one simple explanation: the collapse of Biafra. The stories of the war told and retold by my father were also often laced with different songs with which the soldiers in the trenches used to embolden themselves; lessen the anxiety and unpredictability of warfare or even justify their involvement in the war. However, of all the repertoire of war songs from my father, we loved most the song which tells how a gallant soldier overcame the temptations of the flesh in the form of a paragon of beauty named 'Sheri' who tried to lure him away from fighting the war.

Later on in life, I used to see the Sheri song as telling a story similar to the Biblical account of Eve and the serpent that successfully hoodwinked Adam and enticed him into sin. I equally realized then that Sheri as used in that song, contrary to our belief as kids was not the name of a particular lady but generic for dearly beloved or very pretty woman. However, my father's soldier must have been made of sterner and tougher moral fabric than the Biblical Adam since he easily overcame his own temptation – a woman. The song rendered in vernacular goes:

Ejewe lam ikwaamgbo

117

Sheri shim akwaalamgbo
Akaapukwala Sheri
Sheri, isimgbalaga?
Onyega-akwaanumgbo
Mamugbalagaa?

The above would translate into something like this in English:

I had set out to engage in the war
But Sheri said I should not get involved
May it not be well with Sheri
Sheri, do you really mean I should abscond?
Who will then fight the war
If I listen to you and abscond?

Although he regaled us with different stories of the war and his own brave contributions, the best two which he loves and never gets tired of telling are about the exploits of his unit – the 36th company in the Abagana sector of the war and the supernatural qualities and invincibility of the bearded rebel leader who reputedly had a well-known bunker which nobody can for sure tell where it is actually located. In fact, legend has the bunker located in six different and often contradictory locations within the different geographical areas of the rebel republic. For my father, this bunker reflects the personality of the rebel leader and can be moved from one subterranean location to another depending on security and perceived threat to the life of the rebel leader.

It was the mobility of the bunker that my father saw as the reason why the opposing forces never captured or killed the rebel leader in spite of massive bombardments and the most thorough search for him towards the end of hostilities.

Predictably, I can remember these episodes of my father's war stories because they were told so many times to us as children that we can in fact retell them even backwards.

In my father's estimation, the Abagana sector of the rebel resistance should be considered the epitome of heroism. In a voice often lyrical and deeply throaty at the same time my father retold the exploits of the rebels at Abagana signaling out a particular date as the day the rebel soldiers in that sector showed the enemies how a gallant army should fight. That day, according to him was March 31, 1968. It was the day the federal troops fell headlong into a rebel ambush and suffered the outcome. On that eventful day the rebel troops destroyed ninety-six vehicle convoy of the enemies at Abagana. It was a day the locally made rebel army bomb nicknamed 'ogbunigwe' i.e. that which kills by the hundreds showed its destructive supremacy.

It was also a day on which careful planning, superior strategy and adroit use of hardware tilted the war briefly in favour of the rebels. On each occasion as my father went on with this narration of the carnage suffered by the enemies and the courage exhibited by rebel fighters in facing enemies who had both demographic and hardware advantage that day, one could notice a growing huskiness in his voice and little traces of tears towards the end of the story as he bemoaned the fact that despite the gallantry of Abagana, the rebels still lost the war. It was to him, an instance of the gross injustice of providence.

As I had mentioned earlier, my father was greatly enamored with the rebel leader and saw the rebellion as the most rational option at that point in the history of the nation. His belief in this case was supposed to be taken as pure catechism – you wholly accept it, affirm it and repeat it without adding or taking away any dot because it is sacred testimony. It was not unexpected as such that in some advisory sessions while growing up, my father had positioned the rebel leader as the epitome of greatness and service to one's father land. This was in spite of the fact that my father had other veterans who fought on the rebel side but have almost negative views about the rebel leader and his execution of the war.

These other veterans, that my father would have derisively called "sabo" (short for saboteur), suggested that the rebel leader was inordinately ambitious and guilty of mismanaging an ill-advised rebellion. However these fellows were safe with their convictions so long as they did not utter such blasphemy and sabotage to the direct hearing of my father. I would now believe that some of these people who were friends or associates of my father were well aware of how passionate he can be over this matter and never broached it with him or in his presence. The only one who tried, discovered too late how passionate and personal my father still took this matter even decades after the event. Mr. Bartholomew Okeke was the only unfortunate one.

Bald headed and half-toothed Mr. Okeke used to be a regular visitor to our house as children. Mr. Okeke was a very soft-spoken man who lost his wife early after they had managed to conceive only a daughter. We loved Mr. Okeke or Bartho as my father called him because he was so nice to us children, always visiting with packets of Bonbon sweets or Congo bread for us and serving us these goodies with a beaming smile. We had been told by my father that Mr. Okeke lost half of his teeth during the ad-hoc training session they received in the military camp during the civil war. They were not career military men but had been conscripted into the military to boost the number of fighting men available to the rebels who were reeling from both the superior weaponry and demographic size of the opposing federal troops. The story about his tooth had come in response to my innocent question on why God did not give Mr. Okeke the large number of teeth he gave other adults in spite of the fact that he was such a good man. After all, we had been told that children are the ones with porous cavities since they use their teeth in drinking milk and eating fried bean cake.

The accident that cost Mr. Okeke his teeth was a product of his lack of mastery of the "Shetima" or heavy artillery machine gun which butt had connected with his jaws as he battled to load it, knocking him unconscious and leaving half of his dentition on the sands of the primary school commandeered for the camp. The injury had been taken lightly by both the injured and the trainers as a small distraction. In the heady days of the civil war, such a small incident had been over-powered by the over-running patriotic fervor of the period. Mr. Okeke had been a family friend for years and though he did not serve in my father's revered 36th Company or Abagana sector; he had also seen warfare and like my father had risen to the rank of Sergeant before the end of the war. But such shared history and long standing friendship did not spare Mr. Okeke from my Father's ire the only day he got courageous enough to criticize the former rebel leader. I could still vividly recollect what transpired that evening between the two men as I was in the family living room that time ostensibly engrossed in reading the Bible.

I however cannot recall how the usually animated discussion between the two got to the war but I heard my father's familiar mantra:

"Look, Bartho this country died the moment Biafra collapsed. I know many people believe this but nobody would be courageous enough to say it to those ostriches in power now"

121

"You know you have always said this, but …" Mr. Okeke ventured tentatively

"Yes, but what?" My father asked

"I mean people after all these years have different ideas about how things should have been done. It's like people now do not believe entirely that the war was unavoidable".

"Well, those on the other side have never seen anything bad in the first place with the way our people were treated including even the massive pogroms in the North. After all, it was the injustice which went unchallenged by the powers that be that caused the war. So the war was not just one option but the only option". My father argued, warming up to a subject very close to his heart.

"You know you will be surprised to see that even some of us on the rebel side somehow share the belief that the war was not unavoidable". Mr. Okeke continued, drawing unusual courage somehow.

Perhaps the usual shot of Brandy which Mr. Okeke consumes on visits to our house had somehow become stronger on this day. I thought and glanced at the Brandy bottle on the centre table. It was innocent and full looking as usual.

"I can understand when those who did not fight the war on our side, like women and children say this. But I think all of us who did the things men should do know better". My father continued in his normal disposition of believing in the sanctity of his viewpoints.

"I wish so, but I have my doubts". Mr. Okeke retorted

"I beg your pardon. What are you trying to tell me Bartho?" My father asked raising his voice a pitch higher.

Mr. Okeke should have read the handwriting on the wall at this point and made a hasty retreat to allow sleeping dogs lie.

122

But like the proverbial dog that can no longer perceive the odour of faeces when pursued by death, Mr. Okeke plunged in:

"Like I have thought about the whole thing all these years and I honestly feel that perhaps things should have taken another turn. I mean we did not need the additional burden of diseases, poverty and death of millions to our woes as the war exposed us to".

"This is certainly interesting. Why don't you come out openly with what you think or have you equally lost the courage of your own conviction". My father baited Okeke, obviously spoiling for a fight.

But Okeke fell into the trap head-on. It was like he had gotten tired of drinking my father's brandy and the occasional savouring of the taste of my mother's melon soup.

"I think our leader erred in judgment and took the Aburi thing too far to heart". He paused as I stole a quick glance at my father's face.

The face was horrible, like something stung by a bee and I could faintly hear the soft but regular expulsion of breaths from his nostrils as he tried in vain to rein in his awakening anger. But Okeke either did not notice these physical changes or had concluded that enough damage had been done already to make a retreat now futile.

"Don't get me wrong. Nobody can deny the injustice and we witnessed the carnage of human slaughter and pogrom in the North just before the war. But I honestly believe that aside the Aburi, Ghana meetings and accord, the leader should have exercised more restraint and involved the international mediators more and …."

"Bartho, you know one can never know his friends enough. No wonder the white men inserted the word, sabotage in their dictionary. This is really interesting, indeed". My father said in that ominous lower voice of his.

But Mr. Okeke was already immune from danger today and continued. "There is no need trying to affect this dramatics, just try and reconsider the whole episode, you will...."

Enough was enough for my father at this juncture as he quickly stood up like something ejected from a pistol. I got agitated as I thought he would bounce on the rather diminutive and almost frail looking Okeke but he knew better than raise a hand against his guest. He just dashed to the door within a time frame I am sure would have impressed any Olympic sub-ten seconds indoor athlete, yanked it open and boomed:

"Okeekee, out. You have abused my hospitality enough and please do not ever show your sabotaging and sorry face at my door again. To think that we thought at some point we could have won the war with people like you. Sabo, get out". He almost gave Okeke who had quickly gathered himself and approached the exit a shove on the back.

This was the last I saw of Mr. Okeke as a small boy in our house though my mother told me once when I came home on holiday from the university that she had succeeded in making some peace between the two men. The encounter was one of the few occasions I had seen my father livid with anger and without his usual admirable control of the situation. He was not by any estimation a bad man or even an arrogant fellow; he was just a deeply patriotic man who has never reconciled himself to the stark reality of a lost war in which he gave his all. Perhaps if all those who fought on the rebel side of the civil war were as committed and passionate about the war as my father, the outcome might have been different.

But why bemoan split milk, it never does one any good. My father's only consolation was his belief as a Christian that nothing ever happens without the permission of the Almighty. So ultimately he accepted the fact that the rebellion and events preceding and succeeding it ended the way they did because the Almighty willed them so. In fact as time went on I began to believe that the Biblical quotation which I saw prominently adorning the wall above my father's bed on one of my holiday sojourns as an undergraduate might have been nothing more than his belated attempt to rationalize and deal with the inescapable reality of the outcome of the war. The quotation taken from the Book of Ecclesiastes 9:11 goes thus:

I saw something else under the sun: the race is not won by the swift, nor the battle by the strong, nor does bread go to the wise nor riches to the intelligent; favour is not for the learned, for fortune and misfortune overtake them all.

Nine: Khana's Reminiscence

The cell has gone very quiet, Khana observed. He thought about Jerry Oldo who had become his closest friend in the holding cell; who knows how he is faring now or whatever is his fate now. You cannot just predict these steel helmets. You cannot say what comes next with them. Khana surveyed the cell again, even the dogged man of God who he was just conversing with now was slowly drooling off to the nether world of dream and sleep with his head doing a strange routine of chin up and down every other minute. It was best to shut up and allow the poor guy some time to sleep. Sleeping was of course a very big luxury in the cell and those who put them here had made certain of that, utilizing the two crude methods of maximum discomfort and cell over-crowding. So while there was nobody preventing you from sleeping with a cudgel or any other physical instrument, the layout and ambience of the cell were sleep extinguishing indeed.

Shortly Khana began to hear the slight undulation of deep breaths and soft snores as the inmates succumbed to the hands of nature. It was actually one of the proverbs of the people of the Delta region that sleep is a tool of nature like death and that you cannot get out of paying your debt to them; you might delay the payment and even extend the credit time but ultimately you must pay. Khana saw what was happening now in the cell as eloquent proof of that saying. He has often wondered on the power of local knowledge especially the conventional axioms and proverbs of the people anywhere in the world. The amazing fact is that some of the strangest proverbs or sayings steeped in local knowledge or wisdom often reverberates as truism. This is in spite of how strange, funny or even common the saying appears. Take for instance the proverb that "he who defecates without passing urine owes the land a debt of soup" which sounds very funny and even nonsensical at the same time but which is a curious underlining of the immutable relationship between the various forms of waste discharge in the human body.

As strange as it is, people find it difficult to go through the process of defecation without passing some amount of urine at the same time. Perhaps to do otherwise might be tantamount to offending the guardians of such exercise in the traditional society. But even more interesting is that people use such proverbs to indicate situations when two interrelated actions must go together. For instance, he who gives his hand in marriage must expect the accompanying parenthood and when this does not happen, he owes his kinsmen the explanation on why his marriage has not produced the accompanying and expected result - children. So the individual should not pick offence when kinsmen ask questions or worry about this since he has set himself up for this by getting involved in marriage. Marriage and child birth go together in the traditional belief system.

The more he thought about the overpowering validity of some of these expressions handed down through generations among his people, the more he now appreciated the obvious anguish of one of his general studies lecturers in the university who as a budding professor of African History came to give the students a lecture on eh...what was it again. Yes, "Indigenous Knowledge as Modern Life" or something very close to this on one of the last Fridays of the month. In his university, it was the practice that students in the first and second year who are still grappling with the mandatory general studies courses are exposed to the thinking of the big academics in the various disciplines through the monthly last Friday lecture series.

The ninety minutes special lecture - forty five minutes of lecture and forty five minutes of questions and comments following it – has been rechristened "the monthly Friday boredom" largely by fun loving and fun seeking students who could not wait to get caught up in the usual thank goodness it's Friday mood. Well, the professor of history who is no mean academic going by his accomplishments and popularity sought to prove to students, more than half of who were there in the first place because attendance was compulsory, that in spite of the celebrations of modernity represented by such things as space tourism, fiber optics, I-pads, slum tourism, space tourism, cloud computing, electronic voodooism etc. a lot of people's lives and even a lot of the celebrated markers of the modern world are either directly built from the indigenous knowledge of various peoples in the world or are efforts to solve problems that had earlier been identified in the indigenous knowledge system .

According to him, the modern art of writing is nothing but a critical and time structured elongation of the ancient hieroglyphics of the ancient Egyptians just as space travel remains a model and innovative transformation of the astral travel embedded in some religious forms from the Orient. He went on and on to give instances from different practices and locations in the world on how the modern draws regularly from the old or traditional knowledge systems. His main contention, as I remember now is that if knowledge is rightly incremental then nothing has been lost through time rather innovation and the consumptive and large scale demands of today have in so many instances transformed local knowledge to what we now perceive as modern. In other words, he sees indigenous knowledge as neither "strictly indigenous" nor "local" as some writers would rather have us believe but rather as knowledge with an older provenance than today's knowledge.

The professor's lecture as sound as it would appear to a discerning and attentive audience was not any of the above to the student body listening in various states of delirium and boredom to him. As a seasoned classroom teacher, the professor was acutely aware of the fact that only about ten percent of his listeners were paying any good attention to his prepared lecture. This was what caused him anguish and thus made the last ten minutes of the lecture time for berating the laziness, docility and unwillingness to learn attitudes of today's youth. It was one of the givens of the world that each generation saw itself as better behaved than succeeding generations while at the same time seeing preceding generations as archaic and too conservative to matter much. Incidentally the berating caused more problems as the students sensing the anguish of the lecturer and in typical student fashion decided to become rowdier as a way of ensuring that proceedings were brought to a speedy end. In the above atmosphere the call for questions and comments after the lecture were hardly utilized as the noisy and rowdy students, in overwhelming majority created a mild bedlam that made the professor to hastily retreat from the lecture theatre and seek the quiet solace of his office.

Khana looked around again in the cell. It was a terrible picture since people were caught in un-sleeplike postures but yet were asleep. Khana sighed; he was not feeling any bit of sleep though it must be the wee hours of the morning. He sighed again as his mind went to his early days as a student unionist and the influence of the late Kola Dachima. He could still visualize Kola's ever amiable and friendly face in spite of the fact that it has been three years since the demise of the erstwhile student union leader and human rights crusader. Kola was one of those lucky (or even unlucky, depending on how you see things) people whose complexion or skin colour is a mixture of ebony black and fair without being anything near half-cast. In fact, these days people call them quarter cast (if ever that is correct); though Kola was not very handsome, he had very distinguishing facial attributes – prominent forehead, a pointed nose though wider in the typical African way at the end, well rounded and full lips and a very small set of eyes reflecting a mixture between deep blue and light yellow.

But perhaps Kola's most prominent facial attribute was his perfect finished set of teeth topped off by the crevice between two teeth set in the centre of his mouth. Being a born speaker with the gift of the gab, the open teeth was one of the first things people noticed about Dachima. But for Khana, Dachima was not just a role model but was equally the one who introduced him to student unionism. As a freshman then contesting for the hall elections in his hall of residence, Khana had gone looking for the then already larger than life Dachima who had just assumed office as the President of the university students' union body after having served previously as the secretary general. It had been one of those on the spur of the moment but often intuitive decisions on the part of Khana. He simply needed advice or some sort of guidance from the President who even though he cannot openly support any candidate can subtly endorse any and such endorsement given Dachima's popularity was as good as having won the election. Khana's visit apart from intuition and whatnot was also borne out of fear; fears that he had committed an unpardonable blunder in contesting for an executive position in his hall government even though he was still a freshman. The visit had been hastened all the same by the additional fact that Khana had received a visit on the night before the day of his visit to

Dachima from a group of four final year students resident in his hall. The group called themselves the political elder statesmen and was fully in support of the third year student contesting against Khana.

The visit of the elder statesmen had been very brief, lasting less than five minutes and had taken place in the hostel room Khana shared then with three other students. The group had gone straight to their mission with no ceremonies and not minding that two of Khana's roommates were present. The message delivered by the tallest and meanest of the four was simple: "do you realize you are a first year student in this university. You are doing the unthinkable and unprecedented by contesting the elections. Take our advice and withdraw and wait for your turn. Go ahead and fail and jeopardize your chances of ever making it in the future. Do not say we did not warn you". The group left as they had come – with no formalities or goodbye. Even though Khana had before this time felt the itch to see Dachima, it was this late night visit that made seeing Dachima the first project the next day. As luck would have it, Khana caught him in the student union secretariat as he was getting ready to dash out for a morning lecture. Khana had introduced himself as a first year student and stated why he had come to see Dachima including the visit from the elder statesmen. At the end, Dachima had asked, "are you familiar with the constitution of the students' union?". To which Khana replied, "yes, we got it during registration and I have read through it thrice"

"And who does it say is qualified to contest student union elections here", Dachima asked

"The criteria are: evidence of registration as full time student; course registration for the session; and financial membership of the student union", Khana answered breezly.

"Then are you qualified on these grounds", without waiting for Khana's answer he continued, "I know that you are truly qualified, if not the union electoral body would not have cleared you to contest".

As if reading Khana's surprise, he continued "yes I know about your case. It's like a never happened before case here. So even without meeting you until now I know all about your political aspirations". Dachima paused and Khana interjected, "so what do you think?"

Dachima cleared his throat and smiled, "but let me ask you the big question – what is your motivation for seeking the office?".

"I want to…eh serve. I think I can be of service and I just like politics", Khana offered

"You know this answer would not win you friends or votes but it is a reflection of sincerity and I like that".

Khana was elated and was at the verge of asking whether Dachima supports him, when Kola continued, "but truth never wins elections. While lies can be dangerous; in politics one must always be economical with the truth, avoid the open lies but leave room for escaping from being roped too tight on the pole of the truth".

"I beg your pardon. You have lost me there", Khana commented puzzlingly

"Never mind, you will learn. Anyway, my good friend the law of convention is actually against your candidature since like I mentioned it has never happened before. But the world has moved so far because people were willing to challenge traditions and established positions. Like it is said change only comes when some people resist or challenge the status quo. I mean Obama would not have emerged the President of the US if he had bided his time and waited for tradition to change ", Dachima said looking at his watch.

It was obvious to Khana that his visit was getting to a close, so he asked, "So do you support me or rather do you think I should go ahead and contest?" The reframing of the question was quickly done by Khana as he realized that the union President is not expected to show open support to any candidate. Obviously this realization by Khana won him the admiration of Dachima who said.

"I think you should go ahead my good friend. And remember I wish you the best and come and see me when you win the elections. Goodluck", Dachima said as he gathered his books and moved ahead of Khan out of the secretariat. Even though a busy student unionist and recognized university functionary Dachima prided himself on neither missing his lectures nor coming late to them. His teachers were in love with him for this since it gave them the leeway to use the proverbial stick on the habitual truants.

Khana shifted his weight from one side of the buttocks to the other in the cell and smiled again. That first meeting with Dachima was the beginning of a relationship that lasted the two more years that Dachima had to run in his five year agricultural science degree programme in the university and continued after their student days. Khana had gone ahead to win the elections by a surprising landside and thus began his activist life style. He practically adored Dachima who he still regarded as the most eloquent man he had ever met. Apart from a mere gift of the gab, Dachima had the uncanny ability to rouse even the most docile audience and stimulate them into audacious action in the cause of justice or human rights without directly telling them to act. Khana recalled vividly how on one occasion, Dachima had used this ability to great effect.

It has been towards the end of his first year as a student and the occasion was a student union orchestrated protest against the spiraling cost of food, beverages, stationeries and small consumables on campus. Incidentally and secretly but under the guidance of a local politician-owner of one of the biggest retail shops inside the campus, goods sold on campus including food and beverages had gone up in a very ingenious and systematic way. In this sense, the goods were made expensive but a fraction cheaper than buying them directly by going into town in the sense that what the sellers add on top was the equivalent of the cost of one way transportation to the town. This was unlike the previous case where the goods and food sold at the same price as those in the market and commercial avenues in the town, a mere two kilometers away. The basic logic was that rather than paying for a return trip on a taxi or motorbike to buy the article or eat food in town, the student would gladly pay the fifty percent of the transport cost added to the normal cost of these articles and food on campus. It was smart thinking and was already working out for the business community on campus until Dachima unraveled the mystery behind the overnight campus only inflation that had made goods more expensive.

As usual, the students' grievance was taken to the university administration but given the involvement of the local political chieftain who the then university administrators felt was important in giving them some political leverage beyond the campus town, the administration feigned ignorance of the argument or position of the students. Given that the chief executives of universities are usually appointed on final approval/endorsement given by the political leaders, those in such positions and those aspiring to them see the garnering of as much political leverage as possible as very important. In fact, given pervasive corruption and acute monetization and contamination of the process of selection of chief executives of the universities, those with such ambitions often first build reasonable political connections before airing their intentions or ambitions.

Actually, one of the first questions one is asked on revealing interest in such office is whether he has the needed political clout. Given the lukewarm attitude of the university administration to a genuine students' grievance, the union took it upon itself to do something. That something turned out to be predictably a week of protests and sacking of a good number of the business units that refused to go back to the former price regime. However the high point of the protest was the torching of what was the biggest retail outlet on campus owned by the powerful local politician. It was an act of student impulsive drive neither planned nor led by anybody. The review of the crisis later on by the university administration came to the same conclusion. Therefore no scapegoats were held responsible. But those of us close to Dachima and well aware of his oratory and persuasive powers knew that the outcome of burning the big retail outlet could have been predicted the minute he finished an address some twenty minutes before the incident. Dachima had simply addressed the student body on the information emanating from a couple of small time business operatives on campus who had been harassed earlier that they were simply towing the lines established by the bigger ones especially the outfit owned by the local politician. The inference of the small operatives was that they were being singled out for students' reprisal because they are small and not as influential as the big ones.

So Dachima had gone to great length to disabuse their minds on this and addressed students for the third time in the week of the protest calling their attention to the acts of unrepentant capitalists who in a show of abuse of both the hospitality of the university and patronage of the students have turned the campus into zones for unbridled capitalist pursuit of excessive profit from anybody and anywhere. Dachima continued by arguing that incidentally those who are responsible for this unfriendly act are also those who benefit from the massive corruption in the state and who peddle avarice and greed as political craft. Rhetorically he asked, "Do I need to go on or are we now clear on who the enemy is?" This question was greeted by both cheers and boos as some students cheered Dachima's speech and others at the same time booed at the so-called capitalists who are enemies of the students. Riding the wave of the massive support, Dachima continued, "Seeing they say is believing, why don't we go and see what happens there anyway". And bedlam was let loose as the students marching to the songs of solidarity descended on the politician's outfit.

Khana smiled again, Dachima was something else. Little wonder he had quickly moved into the human rights crusade sector promptly on graduation. Given the massive human rights abuses, injustice and privation visited on a good number of people by a government without the slightest legitimacy, Dachima had felt challenged to give his service. He was after all one of those few people born without the ability to ignore injustice or remain passive to repression for a long time. In the human rights sector, he had risen to prominence and had won international recognition. If that was a career, he was doing well until last three years when he died in a strange circumstance in a freak landing accident on a domestic flight. It was still a matter of conjecture what had really happened since he was the only fatality and he was travelling with some top notch government functionaries.

The unvoiced deduction was that he had been arranged into the great beyond by the agents of the government since he had become an ever blistering wound on the side of the government of the day. Dachima had been lured into accepting membership of a government established permanent panel on ethnic minorities' grievances. A position he had accepted on the belief that it would provide him with a chance to ensure that the right things are done and redress given to those who had been made victims of ethnic marginalization and injustice. It still stands to argument whether he had been given a genuine chance to effect some of the things he canvassed for or whether it has been one big plan to entrap and extinguish him. Whatever, Kola died without saying bye to his newlywed wife and even seeing the child born by his love five months after his death. Khana could feel the tears on his cheeks. Whoever said men do not cry.

Ten: Kinsmen

"Cell zero", a jangling noise roused me from my reverie. Standing in the port hole of my cell door was a guard with a very unfriendly face. I wondered where my good guy had gone.

"Today is Sunday and you are being moved, so get ready', the unfriendly guard announced without much ceremony. I was getting out of solitary confinement and the spiky guard was saying it as if nothing has happened.

I once more wondered why they didn't send my good guard to come with the news, may be it would have been very interesting and cheerful. I have developed a kind of unspoken but deep and warm bond with the good guard.

I followed the unruly and overtly unfriendly guard to the end of the passage and we took a right turn into another passage, at the end of which we came face to face with the grilled door of a cell. On entering the cell, three things recorded in my senses immediately, the light which right from the passage has been playing tricks with my eyes, the noise which I guess might be traffic, and the people already in the cell. There were already seven inmates in the cell boldly labeled 02. Actually it was the size of the standard living room one finds in a commercial flat in most metropolitan towns in the country. Among the seven inmates were five new faces and two of my former associates, Khana and the man of God.

There were eight crusty foams, i.e. beds scattered without any thought neither for order nor interior decoration. There were two little windows set very high, almost to the roof of the room. The windows were a little bigger than hen holes but enough light was streaming through them into the cell and almost slightly from the grilled door. I guess the door was grilled with those sturdy iron bars so as to achieve two things, prevent attempts to get away though I don't think any right thinking person would ever contemplate that in an SSS cell (though peoples' mind eventually get warped by such inhumane incarceration), and to give the guards full view of proceedings in the cell every time of the day or night. They spy on the inmates mostly in the night and the wee hours of the morning.

Immediately I came in, the new five cell mates swarmed on me. They wanted to know if I was just coming from outside i.e. if I had just been arrested. They asked these questions with a lot of excitement which abruptly died off when I informed them I was coming from solitary confinement and had been there for some time. I noticed that Khana and the man of God hung back with a mixture of mirth and smirk playing on their faces.

One very scrawny boy of about nineteen stood around me and helped me make up my own foam with the bug-ridden beddings the guard threw in after me. As he helped stretch one end of the frayed bed sheet I wondered what a young man like that might have done to merit lodging in this 'stately' quarters. So as soon as we finished I started a conversation with him. You can never beat a journalist on that score.

"What is your name, sonny?"

"Cut that sonny stuff, I am Freeman but prefers to be called Freedom", the young man answered.

"Why?" I asked.

"Because it is only after freedom that you can get freemen. The logical thing should be freedom before freeman. And since we are still far from being free, I should answer freedom. That way, the fact that the country is enslaved by a tiny group of military and political elites remains always at the conscious and sub-conscious levels'.

Fine logic. 'But why do you feel we are not free?', I asked.

"Well, if you are free, you wouldn't be here, would you?"

I couldn't help understanding his point of view. Freedom is a whole and immutable ingredient of civilized society. Any society in which the freedom of individuals can be curtailed or entirely erased at will by the powers that be is far from being civilized.

"How old are you freedom?"

"Well, I think it's kind of personal. But since we are all here in the cell despite our personal wishes, I don't think there is anything anymore personal about us. So I am nineteen years old or would precisely be that in about sixty days from now if my brain calendar is right".

My inquisitive nature found out that Freeman a.k.a. Freedom like Khana was from one of the oil producing communities that is fighting for semi-autonomy and compensation from the central government. He had been arrested because of his role as a youth leader in one act of sabotage on oil installations carried out by the youths of his riverine community. He had informed me that security men had rounded up all leaders of the youth forum of his community and that they were being held in various cells in the country. But that no degree of repression, torture or incarceration would break the resolve of the people to fight for what belongs to them.

"But do you think your cause is worth the trouble?" I asked tentatively.

"You see our community is blessed by God who gave us petroleum and other mineral resources, but this black gold has now turned into a source of sorrow for the people. For over twelve years now, no farmer in my place has reaped any harvest, why? Because oil is no longer there. The nonchalant

141

exploitation of oil by the government and their oil firms have left the soil bereft of nutrients. Trees, leaves and grasses have all died off", he paused, swallowing saliva.

Bracing himself up and gesticulating as he would likely be doing if addressing a youth forum, he continued.

"The air people breath is full of dangerous carbons and other pollutants which are choking the lungs and are causes of cancer, skin and lung disorders most of which are terminal in nature. Big drilling holes, excavations, pits and other topographic channels now adorn the surface of the community. You can neither breathe clean air nor walk about freely and to think that we have no other home apart from that. Those greatly affected are the old men and women who are permanently domiciled in the village. They are fast dying off as a result of pollution and exposure to unhealthy exploitative practices of the oil companies. Do you know that my community has the highest old age mortality rate in Africa and the least child survival potentials in West Africa? Do you still think we need further justification?"

"I have heard of all these things before, but I was of the view that your leaders were purposely exaggerating them in order to reap more than commensurate benefits from the government", I explained lamely.

"There is no exaggeration about it. Anytime you get out of this place that is if they allow you to leave alive, take a trip to my place and see terror and horror for yourself. And what have we gained from the discovery of bountiful crude oil in our place? Practically nothing".

"What of the percentage they pay to oil producing communities, the development commissions and the community development efforts of the oil companies?"

"Look a lot of these things are nothing short of propaganda and the practice of deceit by the government. I mean what is the ratio of such government tokens to the degree of destruction in the community? Who receives the said money? Who benefits from the numerous projects of the commission? What efforts are made – I mean concerted efforts by the oil companies to put back a little of what they take from the land?'

Definitely we were discussing an issue very close to the heart of Freedom and in which he has acquired dangerous knowledge. That is, crude truth clothed in the garb of passion. But I was willing to task him over it.

"You mean all these things we hear are lies? That no efforts are made to develop the oil producing communities and that the oil firms do not give amenities to their host communities and so on?" I asked disbelievingly.

"Not exactly but you know that a drop of salt into an ocean makes no difference. The point is that despite what the government, the oil companies and the development commission might be doing they have not made any iota of difference to the people; rather the degradation continues on a worsening scale, people keep on dying and the stench grows, the air becomes a veritable source of death and illness. No, they have not done enough. They have never tried and they have never been sincere with the people".

"So what do you want now from the government?" I asked gradually conceding defeat.

"Nothing short of full compensation and a stop to all forms of mineral exploitation. The oppression of the oil minorities must stop and the people must be fully compensated for all these years of exploitation and the right to self-determination guaranteed to the people".

"So how possible do you think this marvelous solution looks? I know that the mainstay of our economy is the proceeds from crude oil and that the government would not

143

compromise its stand on the issue".

"Well, I don't know about possibility neither can I forecast change. But deep in my soul I am convinced that we are resolved to fight for ever if necessary. No amount of draconian laws, decrees, ruthless repression and use of force would break our resolve to fight for our rights. I am here now, so are many other leaders and spokesmen of my community, I know I might spend a lot of time here now or not come out alive if I give them one slightest justification for that. But I am neither afraid nor moved by such thoughts. The leader who puts self-consideration and comforts first struggles in vain. The struggle is all about sacrifice, pain, privation and finally victory. But before then the struggle must continue ceaselessly. Any relaxation might give the opponents the time to consolidate their offensive. The struggle continues".

"Aluta continua", I chorused after him. In the course of the discourse, Freedom's eyes have turned fiery red and his body was sending out charges of tension. It has long since been revealed and accepted by erudite scholars that nothing brings out the crude determination and dare devil nature in man more than a favourable coincidence of the feeling of ethnic degradation and social injustice. Freedom had spoken with a ferocious fire that would hardly be extinguished and could hardly exist in the heart of other young men. Not only was the struggle his life, it is even his death and his afterlife.

After getting acquainted with Freedom, I was convinced that cell 02 may not be a very bad idea after all. At least not when compared with solitary or other cells where intellectualism and logical reasoning as displayed by Freedom were non-existent.

There were still four other inmates in the cell apart from Freedom who I did not know. I think I better introduce them in order of age. Since I have introduced the youngest, I better

144

go on from the youngest to the oldest.

Next in line was a guy named Johnny Budmi, who is from the South like Freedom and me. Johnny would probably be in his late twenties. With a long face, broad nose and large eyes, he was masculinity personified. Johnny was in detention for a minor act of indiscretion.

He had used his real name in writing a not too good article about powerful government officials. He had timidly sent the article to the official government newspaper – The Daily News. Predictably his article and the various allegations of corruption and impropriety against public officials in it had never seen the light of day. Rather Johnny had been whisked off his seat in the federal treasury department. His article had mainly been about large scale corruption in that department.

Twenty million naira had disappeared into thin air from the treasury. The money had been drawn through irregular and unusual channels. The director of the treasury was involved, so were other senior officials of the department and the secretary in charge of finance and economic planning.

Johnny the patriot had shouted foul and had written an exposure in form of an article to the newspaper. In the article, he alerted the public and the government on the disappearance of the money from the treasury and had pointed accusing fingers at those above him in the office. Ten days after posting the article he was whisked away from his office one sunny afternoon. And since then he had visited three security cells, this being the fourth.

Either he was losing his mental balance or he was suffering from incurable optimism. Johnny still believed that his article would soon be published and that even if that didn't happen, he would somehow be vindicated soon. And all enemies of the state – corrupt government workers and officials would take his present position and a public apology and an even enhanced reinstatement into office would be his reward. Every so often especially in the night pacing from window to grilled door, Johnny would be muttering under his breath, 'the truth will vindicate me … I will soon get out of here a national hero'.

One day, Freedom bored with the prattle had taken him up on that:

"So Johnny when will this your truth and vindication following it take place?"

"Soon, very soon", Johnny muttered in his usual deep and low tone.

He was fond of talking through clenched teeth like a man afraid of being heard.

"When will your soon come? You have been here with us for about a month now plus the other months you have spent some other places yet you talk of soon". Freedom replied.

"You never know and cannot predict the way of posterity. Impatience is often the doom of good fortune".

For me I was sure Johnny was suffering from one or another psychological malady. I have seen it happen before and enough undergraduate psychology classes have taught me to believe it. Johnny although he had spent four gruesome months behind bars was yet to come to terms with that fact. That might explain why he speaks with clenched teeth and is afraid of his voice being heard. Maybe we are all part of a bad dream to him. A bad dream that would soon be over and so don't let anyone hear about it, whenever he wakes up from it, that would be the end and nobody would know.

He was also one of those who bought the ideal so many years ago that our society was fair and that only the bad and evil elements in it are punished. And based on this fundamental delusion he was optimistic that soon the truth shall set him free. But my particular worry was that Johnny was no longer normal, the above notions about his predicament have interfered with his conception and definition of reality. He was an example of the saying that one lives in a dream world. Johnny has mentally constructed a world that exists only in his faculties and more dangerously, inhibits his understanding of the real world he is living in. From the moment the above dawned on me; I decided Johnny was a guy worth watching. You can never tell.

Next was Mustafa Alim, a Northerner of about thirty five or three. With broad tribal cheeks and the aquiline nose so common with the cattle herders of the North and a coffee complexion, Mustafa was a handsome man. However, the stint of hardship in detention had tampered with this God endowed handsomeness. Mustafa is a member of an underground resistance movement. He had been arrested and detained four times previously. On the last trip he had been warned by a popular and rich guardian in Abuja that the next time he goes in, nobody would bother.

Alim is seen generally by people from his ethnic area as a rebel and an ungrateful young man driven crazy by a hopeless ideal, one that had led him to bite the fingers that once fed him. A scion of a royal family, his family and his Abuja guardian had greatly profited from the hegemony in power. He had received free education up to the tertiary level in Switzerland and sent to a diplomatic career in the embassy in the US. There less than three years, Alim had run into members of a socio-religious cult claiming to be modeled after the ideas of the black civil rights hero, Martin Luther King Jr. One year of this intimate association had set Alim on the path of righteous self-realization and questioning of the evil of man and government. He had resigned from the diplomatic career.

"How did your people react to this?" Freedom queried.

"No big deal, as far as am concerned', Alim drawled.

"You mean they just shook their grey hairs and left it like

147

that?"

Before Alim could answer, Freedom cajoled, "maybe they gave you a twenty-one gun salute and a standing ovation for a decision well-taken. Is that what you want us to believe? That it was no big deal as the Americans say?"

"No, there was a big uproar. I mean quite some feathers were ruffled about my leaving a career others were looking for and brandishing political and social ideals that would only remain illusions in Nigeria'. Alim explained earnestly.

"May be they were readying you for a career eventually as an ambassador", I put in.

"Yea, but that is selfish and callous", Alim fumed.

"But I thought every Northerner is tuned regularly to that kind of frequency". Freedom opined.

"Nonsense! That is the stereotype. We, the Hausa and other Northerners know where it pinches. There are those of us with hearts, with some fancy conscience. We also share the ideals and dreams of a better society. Do you know that for every Northern millionaire or power broker you see, there are over two thousand others who are paupers, partially disenfranchised and without future. Go to all the big Northern cities during Salah or any other celebration and see the kinsmen of the President. You will see long lines of beggars, disabled humanity, invalids and pure idiots. They are the sterile and almost morbid remains of a race begging and chanting for the remains from the dinner tables of their privileged kin. Look, poverty and pauperization are worse in the North. People from other parts of Nigeria are either unaware of this or ignore it most times out of the desire to score cheap political points". Alim ended.

"So you are now championing the cause of the talakawas in the North?" I enquired.

"Not at all. I am championing or more accurately wish to

148

champion eh …eh… the cause of the less privileged Naijans in every nook and cranny of this great nation. Look, I still share the optimism of our western friends that with the resource base of this country, poverty and debt should not be nagging issues here of all places".

"So you share their view that Naija can repay her external debts and as a result no debt cancellation for us?"

"I also share a further inconspicuous neo-imperialist interest if you call it that; that Naija should not only pay her debts, but the interests and some fine for defaulting so far".

"That is paranoid", someone from the far corner of the cell hissed. It was

Gerry.

"Revolution is freed by paranoia. Ideals are not worth much it if they don't get the awe of the people and draw the conclusion that the proponent is deranged. So Gerry I'm mad and that is why I am here".

"Jeez, you are going to stay here long". Gerry hissed again.

"For as long as the people, the labouring masses remain chained by miseries and privations, I am content to live here. Any day I live I will fight the oppressors, the hijackers and the robbers of the people's mandate. The architects of mass privation and elite affluence deserve worse. With this in mind, I see myself staying here for long or coming and going. Either way I'm all for it".

"Look, if you overstay here your dream will die with you. No prophet or saviour is worth his salt plus onions if he doesn't change the status quo ante or collect enough followers to do this when he is eventually kaput", Freedom challenged.

"You think I have not taken care of that. For a little more than five thousand Naira, a lot of herders who tramp through the Maiduguri to Umuahia trail on foot herding cattle for Alhajis for peanuts and blistered feet would do more than

149

that?"

Freedom sighed, rose from his corner and whistled. The guards were coming. Their zealous footsteps could be heard on the sweat hardened cobble stones of the penitentiary passage way.

The next cell mate was the Taciturn Gerry; the ebony black, huge and almost effeminate looking Gerry. He has eyes that seemed to be shining always, giving off only one message – innocence. Gerry was amiable to a fault. In the cell, he was the unpaid fence mender and the man to put the lowest spirit in a swing. In fact, Gerry is nothing but a human pick-me up; his effable spirit was as infectious as it was contaminating. He had zero-tolerance for gloom, doom and painful brooding and was ever ready to ignite or fan the embers of joy. Without him and Freedom, it would have been hell. Gerry was in cell for just one reason. His elder brother was purportedly the financier of the last nearly successful coup attempt against the general.

They never caught the brother, the multi-millionaire Chief Briggs but they caught innocent Gerry and two of his sisters. Prior to this, Gerry had been holding down a public relations job in an advertising firm (not owned by his brother) in Lagos. He has not gotten over what he called 'displaced liability', which is making him pay for his brother's sin.

Gerry had come to cell with a passport photograph of his girlfriend which he had hidden in his pants and the frisking hands of the agents had not gotten to it. They were engaged. The girl in the passport was pretty and good looking but to Gerry, she was a paragon of beauty, an amazon of inestimable quality. He hardly makes four sentences without referring to Aisha. He was madly in love and part of his reasoning had been lost to love. Like they say, his grey matter has been contaminated with agape. It is the bane of love; it makes men become half of their brain and power. It breeds distorted personality and a tendency towards absolute imagery. Far away from reality; Gerry's penchant for Aisha and always Aisha while in cell had almost turned him into a sort of outcast in spite of his ebullient nature.

Nobody was ever willing to talk to him or with him because he would certainly bring in Aisha but he could easily draw you into a conversation in spite of your intentions on this score. Even if you did like him which was more like the rule and indulged him in this love fantasy, you soon get bored. When he talks of Aisha, his eyes takes on a tinge of lust, admiration and expectation on a blissful flit to the celestial. Rolling his eyes constantly and swinging his head from side to side, Aisha oozed out of his orifice in various shapes and dimensions.

All the same throughout my stay in the penitentiary at his Excellency's pleasure, there was none more pleasant and gentler than Gerry. A constant source of hope, patience and perseverance, he did a lot by way of his living example and disposition in cell, to make me remain sane throughout that period. Like Alice in wonderland, I still wonder what a nice guy like Gerry was doing in a place like the penitentiary. He was by nature easy going and amiable. Despite the dehumanizing condition of the cell and the incessant torture meted out to him to confess what he knew nothing about, Gerry still carried a smile about the cell even though a wry one sometimes.

There is still a last man to be introduced. With a face chiseled out of mahogany and smoothened by the anvils of an amateur smith, on top of a toady and rough bulging body, he was all he was reputed to be and more than that. A gangland Lord, a Mafioso, undertaker, job man, assassin, coup financier and organized crime business mogul.

Throughout his stay with us, he was thoroughly detached, reticent and obviously aggressive without words. Freedom, the know all and eager friend to all, told me he confided in him that his boys would soon get him out. How they would do this, he never told Freedom and Freedom never bothered to ask. Discretion is always the best part of valour.

His name was Koto Katana and with such a name, I guess all things might be possible. On my first day there in cell 02, one look at his face told me to keep off and I did just that. Amiable Gerry lost a tooth before he learnt to keep off the hard way. Katana was nobody's friend and most peoples' enemy. Freedom once whispered to me in a conspiratorial tone that Katana told him, he had been personally involved in the assassination of not less than twenty people; and was indirectly involved in the death of some forty others. That his oldest rival in whatever business he does now walks with a pronounced limp, one ear and an eye. There may be the element of boasting and even exaggerations in these feats; but he looked and acted the part well enough.

Katana seemed always inscrutable; but a sort of understanding existed between Freedom and Katana. I sometimes believe they knew themselves before meeting in the cell. But one thing I could not fathom was where this commonality of interest lies. Unless freedom had been in some illegitimate deals before being recruited to fight the injustice his people suffers in the country.

Throughout my over four months stay with them in the cell, Katana never laughed once, never sighed and spoke less than fifty words in all. Katana was worth a longer study.

Eleven: Amen, Yes

E xactly two days after my return from the solitary, the whole cell 02 was awoken from whatever groggy state that passes for sleep by the strident screams of "Amen yes" by the man of God who was drenched in sweat and drooling from one side of the mouth even as he was caught fitfully in sleep. We all concluded that the poor fellow has just had a nightmare but he counteracted this on becoming fully awake and rather claimed it was a divine revelation of immense spiritual proportions. I became interested and asked him to reveal this to us, his fellow sufferers. This was in spite of the voiced disinterest of Khana which did not surprise me since I had had the chance of learning his type of spiritual inclination in one of our earlier discussions.

Khana is spiritual to the extent one considers a belief in the traditional deities and their efficacy spiritual or religious. Without doubt, belief in such things are only considered spiritual or religious in academic and such other distinguished circles where the intellect claims to have been released from the intimidating shackles of convention. But in the modern times in which we find ourselves and in which the greater one's distance from the tradition the more urbanized or civilized he is considered, religion has become associated with Christianity, Islam, and to a lesser degree the Oriental and Eastern belief systems. In spite of my Christian upbringing I still wonder why the Oriental beliefs can be rightly labeled modern religion and seen as part of the modern world religions while the beliefs of traditional Africa are castigated and abandoned to extinction.

Anyway even as a nominal Christian devoid of the fire spitting and tongue speaking credentials of so many modern day Christians of the Pentecostal hue, I pitied Khana's lack of Christ in spite of his numerous tribulations. Even though in some remarkable sense, Khana epitomizes the antithesis of many of us since we usually only find a need for God when worldly problems overcome us or we are faced with a problem we cannot solve or a situation beyond our control. Anyway, Khana's objection or not the man of God was determined to let us into his revelation since he said we were involved in it somehow. According to him, the screams we heard were his acknowledgements of the directives from the Almighty regarding the situation of things in the country. Even before giving us the revelation, the man of God said the experience now confirms his strong belief that only divine intervention can thwart the plans of the devil and save the country. Moreover, receiving the revelation in such an undistinguished environment as an overcrowded and stinking cell confirms the Biblical notion that God indeed works in strange and mysterious ways.

The man started his narration by asking if we are all familiar with the popular story of Elijah in the Bible; to which all of us including the irreligious Khana nodded too quick an affirmation. I seriously doubted that we all knew the story of Elijah in the Bible in detail. Speaking for myself, I know largely from secondary school religious classes that he was one of the Old Testament prophets who was sent by God to do one thing or the other among the Israelites. And he was, if I am not wrong the one God sent to the wicked King Ahab who was under the apron strings of his much more legendary wicked wife, Jezebel.

Ignoring our affirmation, the man of God told us that in the dream, God appeared to him in the form of a billowing white cloud of no consistent shape or form and had told him that he was going to be useful to mankind like the Elijah of

154

old. This drew a well-deserved sneer from Khana who only clamped up with rebuking eyes and hiss of "unbeliever" from the man of God. Continuing, he said that God had sent him with a message for the dark goggled General and his cohorts to repent and make reparations for the rape of the economy and stolen lives and privileges. Failure to do so would mean death worse than those of vultures and the wiping out of their lineages from the face of the earth.

The man of God was given ninety days within which to deliver this all important message. Again, Khana lost his patience and asked

"How the hell would you do this, locked up and obviously forsaken in this hell hole?"

To which the man of God replied with condescending eyes "Never doubt the ways of the Lord. Not only will I be out of here in no time. He will certainly make a way for me to deliver His message".

"So how and where do we come into the picture since you said we were involved from the beginning of your narration?" I asked in the nicest voice I could muster.

Before he could answer, the irrepressible Khana butted in again.

"Look, I will advise you to let this remain what it is, a dream or else you will rot here. Don't just try any funny evangelism with these military chaps or you may become history".

Predictably the man of God reacted as any well-groomed Pentecostal would in similar circumstances. He hissed, "Holy Ghost fire. The devil is a liar", and turning to the nearest wall took off on the longest and most passionate prayer journeys I have ever witnessed. I was not too happy with Khana, he should have allowed the man have his fun. Given that this was the longest and most open exchange we have had with the man, I doubted there would ever be another opportunity.

There is gainsaying the fact that the so-called revelation or dream of the man of God may be subject to serious doubt and debate especially on the possibility of the Almighty broadcasting straight to mere mortals who are no longer living in the age of Moses. And I knew that in addition to the vocal Khana, others in the cell judging from their countenance did not believe a shred of what he said, it still rekindled my memory towards a recent book I had read. It was a book I read some months prior to my detention in order to write my monthly feature article for the Diaspora magazine, Africans outside Africa (AoA). Writing for this magazine was one of the few moonlighting exercises I engaged in. This is part of efforts to put some extra quid into my pocket each month. Needless to say that the journalist class in the country was not a well remunerated one.

Actually I see the high rate of corruption or the brown envelope syndrome among a good number of colleagues as the fallout of the grossly inadequate remuneration package plaguing the media houses. As poor as the remuneration of the average journalist was in my own establishment, it was still considered among the best in the country. This says quite a lot about what people earn on the average for all the hard work. Anyway, I had been informed by the editor of the AoA that my contribution for the month in question should focus on the amazing growth of the Pentecostal churches across major African cities and how this was impacting on the membership of the old orthodox churches.

In addition to speaking with a few Pentecostal pastors and informers I had gone through some literature. One of the books I had read which made quite a remarkable impression on me, perhaps because of my catholic background was the collection of essays by a group of people who had converted to Catholicism as adults entitled "Surprised by Truth" edited by Patrick Madrid and published in 1994 by Basilica Press, San Diego USA. The contributions in the book were so interesting that instead of reading the one or two chapters I initially intended in order to grasp the rare incidence of the counter pull from the Evangelical and Pentecostal sects to the mainstream and orthodox churches, I went through the entire eleven chapters within 48 hours. But the one that made a lasting impression on me was the contribution by Paul Thigpen especially where he tried to elucidate the nature of the Catholic Church as the oldest and most consistent in its theological foundations. In this contribution he argues much like the subsequent chapters that unlike the other old denominations that have succumbed to the spirit of the age or embraced change on one critical issue after another, Rome has remained firm on such things as the sanctity of life; nature of sexuality; the supernatural foundations of faith; the essence of God; and the identity of Christ.

I actually would not know how clean or valid these points would come out if subjected to rigorous disputations by those from other denominations even though as a born Catholic it gladdened my heart to note that some people are finding certain things exciting and wonderful about the faith. Perhaps, my fascination with the book and other religious literature for that brief period can be traced to my considerable ignorance in such matters. For someone whose knowledge of the Bible is restricted to the popular catechism class John 3 verse 16; reading others with such extensive knowledge of theology, the scripture, and church history was really intimidating.

Twelve: Looking Up Freedom

Given his better knowledge of the murky and shadow worlds of state detention, it was the activist Khana who alerted us to the fact that the other side of the block where our cell is housed also houses a smaller female holding cell. The idea of a detention cell did not shock me since one had gotten accustomed to the fact that there are women prisons or prison sections for women who had fallen foul of the law one way or the other, but to imagine the treatment of women in the same way male political prisoners are treated here gave me the shudders. This was in spite of my belief that the student female activist Sarah Finih must be in one or another dungeon of the government. How else would you explain her sudden but prolonged disappearance from the public radar? But Khana was very sure of his facts and told me that just like the men – us, there are also women seen or perceived by the government as dissidents and enemies of the state.

He went on to inform me that one prominent female prisoner on the other side separated by the reinforced wall of our cell was the popular female activist Halima Bunu. According to him, Halima had been whisked away from the offices of her NGO in the ancient Northern city some two weeks before Khana's arrest. I could hardly believe this as I knew Halima well enough and was very much familiar with her work. Halima was a core and unrepentant advocate of women's rights and to the best of my knowledge does not pose any real threat to the steel helmets in power. But at the same time, do these people act on the basis of the fact or on the basis of whatever fancy catches them any time. It was horrible to think that people like Halima could also be in similar situation with us but Khana's story gave some respite to our worries about the sporadic noises and pitched screams which often penetrate the walls in the dead of the night. Perhaps the pitched screams and muffled weeping were the signatures of torture and frustration. For me Halima Bunu was one of the most outstanding young women in the country and deserves nothing but national commendation for all she stood for.

Halima was one of the foremost campaigners against female circumcision in the North. The circumcision of females in many societies in the North was an age old tradition which as tradition teaches has the combined virtues of reining-in a girl's libido as well as making her deliver babies easily without complications whenever she marries and is due for this sacred duty of womanhood. Incidentally, female circumcision or what development workers these days call female genital cutting and even mutilation (by those very offended with traditional practices) is of an older existence than even the religion of the people often wrongly seen as starting the practice. While traditional believers did not possess any scientific proof of a relationship between lack of circumcision and sexual promiscuity, they were convinced that the un-blunted female organ is highly sensitive and could easily expose a growing girl to the desires of the flesh before marriage.

These societies hold on to the practice as one of the key rites of passage of young girls into womanhood and marriage. It was also a matter of a cherished tradition handed down from generation to generation. It was still a matter of conjecture the nature of crime committed by Halima that attracted the attention of those in power. However, many observers including Khana would attribute it to a recent interview that she granted to the Times of London in which she alleged that a huge grant received from the WHO for the female circumcision project in the country had been misappropriated by one of the key allies of the President, an army colonel and serving governor of one of the states in the North. Perhaps, Bunu was in incarceration because there was need to teach her that those in power were sacred cows beyond reproach.

The Bunu interview with the Times had been syndicated by two national newspapers and had generated a short-lived groundswell of agitations by civil society groups for a war on corruption among the senior ranks of the military. Incidentally she hails from the same local government area as the dark goggled General cum President and Commander-in-Chief. In fact, unconfirmed rumour has it that both of them have some kind of distant blood relationship though in a typical African society where everybody in any given village is a blood relation of the richest man from there, one cannot tell for sure how near to the truth this was. After all, success measured crudely in our own clime by the amount of money one possesses cannot be an orphan.

I had struck a relationship – exchanging occasional emails now and then and getting invitations to her NGO programs – with Halima after interviewing her about two years ago while doing a relief assignment for the indisposed health and human interests' section editor. I had interviewed Halima as part of a series on health challenges of typical rural dwellers in the country. Incidentally Halima Bunu did not fit my image of a person engaged in such mundane and perhaps arcane issues as female circumcision. Halima is an Oxford educated economics and management graduate; strikingly beautiful in the tall, elegant and graceful Fulani fashion and the daughter of a renowned wealthy family in the North. Her father had made his money as a Kola-nut merchant in the pre-independence era in the ancient city of Kano. The interview was as revealing about Halima's personality and motivations as it was for my knowledge of female circumcision in the country. As it were,

Halima gave me my first good knowledge of what female circumcision is and its nature and consequences and provided materials for a newspaper series that ran for a good one month.

While aware of the largely traditional origin and religious support for the practice, Halima told me that it was how this rite is performed and its consequences for the young girls who go through it that terrifies her and drives her on. According to her, the cutting is regularly performed without anesthetics and under septic conditions by old women who neither have knowledge about human anatomy nor medicine. This is in spite of the fact that circumcision can cause permanent health problems and even death through bleeding.

In fact, Halima in her penetrating narrations got me to wholly share her view that female circumcision is nothing but a ritualized form of child abuse and violence against women. As would be expected, Halima's work had gotten her enviable international recognition. Thus she is the only woman from the North of the country in the influential Inter-African Committee against Harmful traditional Practices (IAC). This organization works with national committees to bring the harmful effects of female circumcision to the attention of African governments and push for appropriate legislations and activism against the practice.

Halima was also energized in her activities by the perceived uniqueness of the practice in the country. According to her, the annoying thing about the practice here is that unlike the situation in such other places like Somalia, Mali, and even Egypt the groups in the North carry out the procedure on girls at the tender age of four to twelve years. However unlike the cases from such other places like the Sudan and Somalia, the North largely favours the 'Clitoridectomy' which is the cutting away of part or the entire clitoris. Halima's technical knowledge of the matter was very refreshing and shows a high level of commitment and devotion to a chosen cause. She had produced highly illustrated posters depicting the harmful effects of the practice and debunking the traditional values ascribed to it.

One key part of this is the one which shows that the practice severely contracts the vaginal passage and makes child delivery tougher and more painful for women. Another showed that the practice could lead to such health problems as hemorrhage, urinary tract infections, and severe labour and even infertility. These posters were done in both vernacular and English. Relying on her knowledge of her people and a smart but acute sense of one's environment, Halima did not make the fact that circumcision can limit sexual pleasures an issue in her campaigns and advocacy.

Recalling all these in my cell now, I fervently prayed that the steel helmets would be persuaded by the international attention Halima's detention would have attracted to let her go without any major damage to her personality or psyche and belief in the goodness of the human race. She needs to be in the field in the North among local communities doing what she does best for the good of humanity.

****

My interrogation and so called black charges against me evaporated one day. I was called by the Deputy Director of Security Services, my back dusted and with a smoke conditioned toothy smile, he told me to go away and out. But that was not all; my detainers had the polish and courtesy to drop me at a friend's house with their unmarked official salon car. It was unbelievable. I was free. Have you ever contemplated what freedom really means?

Freedom means so many things to different people. A

classmate of mine in school saw freedom as the ability to wake up whenever one likes without fretting about either lectures or not preparing enough for an examination. For Freedom, my cell mate, it means the transformation of the socio-economic realities of the oil producing communities. The sociologist, Auguste Comte, defines freedom thus: to be free is not to do what one pleases; it is to be the master of oneself, to know how to act with reason and fulfills one's duty.

Don't bother contemplating freedom unless you have been deprived of it through incarceration in a model third world penitentiary under a dictatorial regime. If you are somebody in Aristotle's line of business, you might go philosophical. But you would end up with a lot of semantics and remote logic bothering on ethos, principles and the fabled rare realities of existence. But take it from the grooves of experience, nobody contemplates or understands freedom more than a former jailbird. But get it clear, every man that has gone through the four walls of a prison for whatever reason and for however short a period (even a weekend jive) qualifies for the jailbird tag. Discrimination shortens this life.

Freedom is the ability to appreciate the lofty position of a man among other animals on this universe. It is not going about your business; to make "my fellow countrymen" type of speeches or to eat your favourite cake and still eat it. It is your ability to give good meaning to the existence of fellow human beings and to preserve the environment. An interest in putting humanity first, a spirited effort to live above board and to sympathize with those whose use of limbs and environment have been curtailed either by omission or design.

More primordially, freedom entails the ability to sleep freely, wake leisurely and snap at every unwarranted visitor. It is that security that arises from the knowledge that you have not stepped on any toe or soiled your fingers and also your soul through some 'deals'. I wonder how many people enjoy this rare privilege in this country today.

I remember my bosom friend, Tony who used to be in the advance fee fraud syndicate a.k.a. 419. Tony had four hefty Alsatian dogs in his compound, plus quite a number of tough looking bodyguards that a typical autocratic President of any banana republic would envy. In addition to these, Tony had a high technology closed-circuit monitoring device which covered his whole compound and a considerable expanse of the neighbourhood. Visitors are thoroughly checked by concealed metal detectors, frisking hands of tough goons and an electronically controlled gate. But all these do not qualify as freedom, though the crime tycoon had more than enough rolls to dole out and spend on the most irrelevant and whimsical of fancies.

But nemesis eventually came, though it did not get Tony. But it got his pretty wife Naomi. She was gunned down by a spray of bullets from a speeding car as she stepped out of a neighbourhood supermarket. Two of her bodyguards were also fatally caught by the hail of bullets. Tony never recovered fully, less than two months after Naomi's tragic demise; he sold out and went to the Caribbean to sojourn. But over there, will he really be a free man with freedom of the soul and the spirit?

Freedom is the ability to take a retrospective look into your life and end up with a smile on your face. But a lot of people I know these days neither smile nor brighten up when brooding over the past. It is always a face contorted like an unpaid worker on protest, and the confused visage like that of a child unable to repair a favourite toy. Sometimes it is a canny and devilish smile like a thug on a dubious prowl. Freedom is also the ability and nerve to visit your relations and kinsmen (if you care for such things) and look them in the eyes, talk earnestly with them and go out of their presence with your conscience

165

unscathed.

Conscience; what is this guy talking about you might wonder. Who has got that these days? A lot of people; but I share the sentiment in certain quarters that some people lack conscience. Is it possible? My aunt would rather argue that people have a dormant rather than active conscience. Whichever way, my logic is that the moment your conscience allows you to do a great evil – duping, murder, armed robbery, blackmail, and other acts like these - you have no conscience, dormant or sleepy. I know that most evil doers are not totally happy because their conscience never allows them to sleep well, enjoy well or appreciate the world.

Granted that, but I would rather say such people are bothered by perennial guilt complex and like rats in a pussy cat alley are bound to be edgy, cagey and touchy. But anybody that his conscience allows to do any great evil hasn't got that often misused and misunderstood judge.

Enough ranting.

I regained my freedom (yes I have always had one). At first I thought it was because of the magnanimity of the government but less than four hours after release, Ordia told me a new government was in power. That might explain my release. It was the next day over lunch that I was given details of events in the country by Umar and Ordia. The banter started from the change of government. Umar and Ordia are both professional colleagues of mine as well as good friends. They were the ones who did all the running around while my incarceration lasted. It was nice giving them the first chance of socializing with me immediately after release. To them, I had achieved some form of stardom from going to prison.

The unconfirmed story is that the new government in power was planning to fish out those of us who had been wrongly jailed and turn us into emergency heroes. That would certainly gain them considerable political mileage. Nothing works better for a legitimacy seeking new regime than having to show-off good citizens who paid the price for bad governance as prisoners of conscience and political prisoners. Perhaps, someone with enough grammar amongst the new men in power would gravely intone, 'they sacrificed their freedom so that we would have a better country'. Hilarious indeed.

As I sat hunched over my lunch of green tuna salad, I envisioned the very likely fact that soon after playing the hero and nice guys' game, the new henchmen in power would start collecting their own batch of political prisoners and all. It is usually a cyclic game in this country where evil, ruins and putrid malfeasance never cease. Like a poorly choreographed circus, where one bad show follows another equally bad one in no particular order, the country is engaged in the ruinous dance of madness at the altar of corruption, larceny and 'kleptocracy'.

Printed in the United States
by Bookmasters

Printed in the United States
By Bookmasters